A VERY MARIAN CHRISTMAS

A MADE MARIAN NOVEL

LUCY LENNOX

CONTENTS

Cover Art by: AngstyG www.AngstyG.com

Editing by: Hollie Westring at www.HollieTheEditor.com

Beta Reading by: Leslie Copeland lcopelandwrites@gmail.com

KEEP IN TOUCH WITH LUCY!

For Sarah MacLean who told my sister I should quit dicking around with MF and write MM. Well, those may not have been her exact words, but they turned out to be the permission I hadn't realized I'd been waiting for. I started writing Borrowing Blue that weekend, and that's where I met the Marians.
(And before you ask, no, I haven't published my MF.)

I had so much fun writing this book, and none of it would have happened without the kick in the pants I got a year ago to start down this road. Thank you, SarahMac, for the timely advice and for writing strong heroines and smart romance.

THE MARIAN FAMILY

Thomas and **Rebecca** Marian

Their children (oldest to youngest):

Pete, married to **Ginger**

Jamie (meets **Teddy** in *Taming Teddy*)

Blue (meets **Tristan** in *Borrowing Blue*)

Thad (dating Tristan's cousin **Sarah**)

Jude (meets **Derek** in *Jumping Jude*)

Simone (dating **Joel Healy**)

Maverick (meets **Beau** in *Moving Maverick*)

Griff (meets **Sam** in *Grounding Griffin*)

Dante (meets **AJ** in *Delivering Dante*)

Ammon (gets rescued in *Delivering Dante*)

Aunt Tilly - Thomas Marian's aunt

Non-Marians:

Granny - Tristan's grandmother

Irene - Granny's wife

Harold Cannon - Tilly's boyfriend (first appears in *Delivering Dante*)

Noah (appears with **Luke** in *A Very Marian Christmas*)

Ben (Griff's biological brother, meets **Reese** in *Made Mine*)

Gideon (Ammon's biological brother)

PROLOGUE

Late November - The Marians

"Sam, next time keep your sausage to yourself. My mouth is still burning."

Griff's head whipped around, and he glared at his brother-in-law Teddy. "What the hell?"

Teddy threw his head back and laughed. "Aww, you jealous, kitty cat? You jealous your husband fed me his spicy—"

Jamie clamped a hand over Teddy's mouth from where he sat snuggled up to him on the sofa. He didn't even look up from his Kindle, muttering, "Jesus," while the rest of the Marians sitting nearby laughed.

It was the night after Thanksgiving. The Marian clan was spread out around the collection of sofas and chairs by the huge stone fireplace in the lobby of the vineyard lodge. Bellies were stuffed with leftover turkey and casseroles as well as some fresh dishes Sam had been testing out for the restaurant. Livers were pickled with enough wine to sink a ship, and many of the Marians were buzzing happily in their post-food stupor. Thomas and Rebecca had long since taken all the grandbabies to bed, and Aunt Tilly, Granny, and Irene were busy arguing over who would win a fight between Audrey Hepburn and Marilyn Monroe.

"Wonder if JFK had a nice sausage," Granny mused into her poker hand.

"Marilyn had tits and a good thirty pounds on Audrey," Tilly said, flipping over another card on the river of their Texas Hold 'Em game. "Plus, she was a spiteful thing."

"Audrey was taller. More likely to use her fingernails and fight dirty," Irene muttered, throwing her hand in.

"I'll bet Marilyn knew how spicy JFK's sausage was," Granny continued, placing down a full house and eliciting a groan out of Aunt Tilly.

Dante and AJ sauntered out from the back hallway where their room was located, trying not to be noticed.

"Again?" Simone called out across the lobby. The pair froze midstep, poor Dante blushing deep pink. "Can the two of you lovebirds go one full hour before sneaking off for a booty call?"

AJ responded smoothly. "Dante had something stuck to his pants."

Pete barked out a laugh. "Yeah, I'll bet he did. Your hands. Nice try there, AJ."

"Oh my god," Dante muttered, hurrying to find a seat and get out of the spotlight. AJ followed him, grabbing Dante up from the over-stuffed chair before sitting his own ass down and resettling his fiancé on his lap.

"Can you blame me? Look at this guy. Plus, what do you expect after all the sex toys you guys forced on us this afternoon?" AJ asked with a grin. Dante tucked his tomato face into AJ's neck to hide from his siblings' teasing.

"You complaining about your impromptu bachelor party?" Pete's wife, Ginger, teased. "Because I thought it was killer."

AJ laughed. "Sally the Love Junk Lady? Really? Poor Dante's face is so flushed right now, I'm afraid he's running a fever."

Griff grinned and sat forward from where he'd been leaning back against Sam's broad chest on the sofa. "Oh, come on. We had to. That's how you two got together, after all. It's tradition."

"We've been engaged for less than forty-eight hours," AJ said.

Simone snorted. "Teddy wanted an excuse to see Sally's new Magic Manhandler. It was all his idea."

Teddy began to make a naughty gesture with his hand, as if demonstrating the Manhandler, but Jamie reached out and grabbed his wrist before he could get a good rhythm going. "Save it for later, hotshot," Jamie said with a laugh.

Derek looked up from where he'd been running his fingers through Jude's hair where he lay in Derek's lap. "I was impressed with the new stuff. Figured we already owned everything good she sold, so that was a pleasant surprise. Can't wait to try out the—"

"Lalalalala," Jude blurted. "Nobody wants to know what you want to try out, big man. Except maybe me, and you can whisper it in my ear."

Derek leaned down to whisper in his husband's ear, and Jude seemed to get extra wiggly in response to whatever words were spoken. It probably wouldn't be long before Jude had something stuck to his own pants.

"What about that cutie-patootie who came with her? Her new assistant, what was his name?" Ginger asked.

Twelve Marian men blurted out at once. "Noah."

The room went silent.

"My, my," Aunt Tilly said with a catlike grin. "Isn't this an interesting development?"

Blue blushed and turned to his husband with an apologetic look. "What? The kid's adorable. You can hardly blame a guy for noticing."

Tristan leaned over and brushed a kiss on Blue's temple, murmuring, "Agreed."

"I'd do him," Beau mumbled into Mav's shoulder. "Sorry, Mav."

Mav turned and kissed his head. "Babe, I thought you were asleep. And you can only do him if you invite me along."

"I was asleep. But then I heard the subject of that hottie come up and had to participate in the discussion."

"Who else would do him?" Simone asked with a mischievous grin. In addition to Simone, Ginger, Tilly, Granny, and Irene, every single gay man in the room except Dante raised his hand.

"I win!" AJ declared. "I have the only loyal partner here. Love you, Dante Marian."

Dante shot AJ a look. "And what about you, jackass? You raised your hand."

AJ had the decency to look ashamed. "I'd just be using him for sex, baby. You know you're the one who holds my heart. Isn't that all that matters? Did you *see* the guy's ass? I mean, come on."

"It was a stellar ass," Irene said sweetly while she shuffled the cards.

"I'd peg it," Granny said cheerfully. "Plus, now that he's working for Sally, he can supply his own peg, so that's a bonus."

"I don't think you call it a peg," Blue suggested. "It's still just a dildo."

"Whatever. Semantics," Granny muttered, flapping her hand at her wife to pick up the pace on the next deal.

"Did you see how nervous and embarrassed he was?" Dante asked. "The poor kid. I felt sorry for him. I'm not even sure he'd seen some of those products before. It seemed like he'd been plucked from a farm in Nebraska and brought here without any preparation. "

"He seemed to know plenty about preparation when he was demonstrating the lube options," Teddy added suggestively. Jamie elbowed him in the ribs.

"No, dude," Beau said. "He really did just move here from bumfuck. Somewhere in Canada, I believe. That's why he looked terrified."

"Aww, poor little Noah. We should introduce him around," Simone suggested. "It can't be easy moving to a new place and not knowing anyone. The kid needs friends."

"Fuck friends," Teddy said. "He needs to get laid. That guy was wound up tighter than Jamie here the night I met him."

Jamie turned blazing eyes on his husband. "Are you fucking kidding me right now? I don't remember hearing you complain that night."

Teddy's own eyes sparkled as he gazed at Jamie. "Ahh, there he is. Feisty Jamie. It's been a while, sweetheart. You've had your nose in that textbook all week. I was just trying to get your attention. Sister and I have been feeling neglected lately." He leaned down and pressed a soft kiss on Jamie's mouth, immediately melting whatever ire Jamie had been brewing. At the sound of her name, Sister's thick black tail beat a rhythm on the floor at Teddy's feet.

"Gross," Simone scoffed. "But he's right. I talked to Noah for a while when we were helping Sally pack up the car, and he said he made the move to the West Coast after a nasty breakup a couple of weeks ago. It sounds like he's looking forward to being single in the city and playing the field."

"Bullshit," Derek said with a laugh. "That guy has serial monogamy written all over him."

"Agreed," Jude said. "It's a shame, though. Plenty of guys would love a turn with that cutie. My friend Baker would be perfect for him."

"Oh my god, he totally would," Derek said, eyes widening. "We should set them up."

"No way," Ginger cut in. "Remember Tall, Dark, and Handsome from Pete's firm? He'd be perfect for our little Noah."

Pete shook his head. "I'm not sure I like where this is going." Ginger shot him a look, and Pete closed his eyes in resignation.

"You all can forget it. Dibs. We're totally setting him up with Hayworth," Maverick said with a grin. "They're both new to town and would be great together." Beau nodded his head enthusiastically.

"Oh, that reminds me, you know who else is new in town?" Jamie asked Teddy. "Did I tell you Josh from Denali was just reassigned to Alcatraz?"

"I always knew that perv would wind up behind bars," Teddy said with a wink.

"Shut up. Alcatraz is run by the park service. Anyway, we should totally set him up with Noah. They're both so sweet."

Teddy's eyes narrowed. "I'm not sure I like you calling other men sweet, doll."

Jamie swooned and stared moony-eyed at his husband for the rest of the conversation.

Dante appeared deep in thought before crying out, "I got it! I'm going to set him up with Jordan from the vet clinic."

Simone shot daggers at him. "That was going to be my pick. Choose someone else."

AJ sat forward, pulling Dante close to his chest and pointing an accusatory finger at Simone. "No way. He picked Jordan first, so he gets him. Don't mess with my man or I will take you down, woman."

Simone pouted and turned away before whining under her breath. "Then who the hell am I going to pick? You people are the ones with all the gay friends."

AJ shot a conspiring wink at Dante before speaking. "Oh, Simone. You know who you should totally set that kid up with?"

Simone's eyes lit up. "Who?"

"Joel Healy from On Your Six Security."

Derek bit his tongue to keep from barking out a laugh.

"Isn't he—" Jude began to ask.

"Gorgeous and successful?" AJ jumped in to keep Jude from saying the word *straight*. Jude looked over at Derek, but Derek squeezed his husband's hand to shut him up.

"I thought he was straight," Simone said, unsure.

"Nope. The guy loves cock. Ask anyone. Ask your brother," Derek assured her before turning to his spouse. "Jude, baby, tell her."

Jude shot him a look before facing his sister and smiling sweetly. "When Derek says he loves cock, he's not kidding."

Derek's nostrils flared in amusement, and it took all of his self-control not to burst out laughing. "Truer words have never been spoken. AJ, bud, did you need a glass of ice water? You look like you might choke."

AJ hid his face behind Dante's head in an effort to keep from cracking up.

Simone still looked confused and... something else. "Wait. Joel Healy is gay? Really? I... *damn*."

Derek lifted his eyebrow at her. "Why do you sound disappointed?"

"Well... it's just that he's... cute. And... you know... nice. You know?"

"No, sister," Blue said with a laugh. "We don't know. Enlighten us. Are you saying gay men can't be nice?"

"Shut up, Blue," Simone snapped. "I just thought a smart, successful guy like Joel Healy would be dating a supermodel or something. Even if he's gay, I'd assume he's taken. Every time we've talked, I thought he was..." She appeared to be thinking things through. "I just thought he was straight, that's all. Are you sure he's gay, I mean... single?"

"He is definitely single," AJ said carefully. "The other day at work I was going on and on about Dante. Joel sounded envious, like he wished he had someone special too."

"Hm," Simone said quietly. "That's kind of sad. He deserves someone special. He's a sweetheart."

"Hot as hellfire too. Back to this dildo kid though. We should place bets," Granny suggested.

Aunt Tilly grabbed for Granny's arm. "Holy hell on a hockey stick, you're right."

"Duh," Granny said before throwing back the rest of her wine.

Irene smiled at her wife before placing down a winning hand with a flourish. "Poker," she declared.

"I think you're thinking of bingo, old lady," Granny grumbled. "Fine, take my money. I'll take it out of your ass later."

Tristan made gagging sounds and tried to hide his face in Blue's shirt. Blue ignored him and heartily agreed with Granny's suggestion. "We should! We should totally place bets, make it a game. The person who sets him up with the guy he falls for wins the pot."

"I'm in," Simone blurted. "Let's do this."

"We can't tell the poor guy he's part of a bet," Ginger said with a grin. "He'd die of embarrassment."

"No, of course we don't tell him," Mav said. "We just all offer to help him meet people in town, and if he so happens to fall head over heels for Hayworth, I mean, one of our friends, then so be it."

"What's the prize?" Derek asked. "It's gotta be something good."

"Season tickets to the Forty-Niners," Ginger suggested gleefully. A room full of Marians stared back at her in silence. "Fuck. Tough crowd. How about tickets to that new drag club?" The room erupted in happy chatter.

"Now you're talking," Teddy said with a grin.

"Nah, it's the pot of money, you bozos. No one has time to shop for an extra prize this time of year," Simone said. "Who wants in?"

They all clamored for a spot in what became known as the Great Holiday Setup, or what Granny insisted on calling OPAH, Operation Pimp-a-Ho.

Regardless of what anyone called the plan, it was decided. They'd invite Noah to bring a date to Marian Christmas, and the couple whose friend was chosen would be declared the winner. No one was allowed to let Noah in on the secret plan, and they only had a month to make him fall in love. Each participant got only one attempt, and they had to do it under the guise of introducing him to new people to help him assimilate to the area.

As they got into bed later that night, Blue turned to his husband, Tristan. "This whole idea is crazy. Nobody falls in love after just one date. Bringing someone to Christmas is a big step."

Tristan reached for Blue and drew him in for a cuddle. "Baby, I pretty much fell in love with you the night we met and haven't been able to get you out of my mind since. When you know, you know."

Blue's eyes sparkled up at Tristan from where he rested his head on Tristan's chest. "Smooth talker. If I didn't know better, I'd think you wanted to get into my pants."

"I do. I sooooo want to get into your pants," Tristan admitted with a sheepish grin. "Been imagining getting into your pants all day, as a matter of fact."

"Prove it."

Within moments, Blue and Tristan were reminded of just how quickly two people could lose themselves in one another when it was meant to be.

1

NOAH

During the entire drive back to the city, I thought for sure Sally was going to have to pull over and force me to stop, drop, and roll to put out the fire on my face. I was beyond mortified.

Sex toys?! I sold *sex toys* for a living?

Had I really moved more than twenty-five-hundred kilometers away from home to take a job selling dildos? I couldn't even say the word out loud.

When I'd had the phone interview with Sally, I'd thought she sold kitchen supplies. She described fun home parties with groups of women and said she needed help branching out into the LGBT market. For god's sake, now I understood what she'd meant. She'd needed a gay guy to sell dildos to dudes. *Dear god.*

There was no getting around it. I had moved to San Francisco to sell sex toys.

I didn't dare tell a single soul.

When I'd met Sally in person earlier that day and discovered the true nature of what kind of products she sold, it was on the tip of my tongue to bow out. I didn't really need the job, after all. I was a registered nurse, just waiting for my license to transfer from Canada before I started a job at a local emergency room.

But she'd looked at me with her big brown eyes and I did what I always did—smiled and nodded. I was a people pleaser. No wasn't in my vocabulary.

I thought back on the group of people I'd just met. The Marian family had been amazing. At least I hadn't been thrown into the deep end on my first go. It could have been much, much worse. I imagined some of those parties were full of drunk partygoers making all kinds of lewd suggestions and gestures with the products, but the Marian family had been relaxed and friendly without putting me on the spot. And since it had been my first event, Sally had done all the talking. I'd listened and learned.

And boy, had I learned.

Growing up in Cold Lake, Alberta, I'd been what most people would call sheltered, but what I would have more likely called lost. As much as I loved my small hometown, I hadn't felt like myself there. I hadn't fit. I'd known since age twelve I needed more. But when it was time to go, I'd wound up falling for a guy who was perfectly content to keep me in Cold Lake forever. So I'd stayed. And stayed. And stayed.

Until I decided enough was enough. Thankfully, I'd known my older brother's childhood best friend, Luke, was living in San Francisco and would be willing to take me in for a little while, so I'd jumped at the chance to finally make my move.

Luke.

What the hell was I going to tell him about my new job? Damn. There was no way I could tell him the truth. I'd rather die. In fact, I probably *would* die. My face would finally explode and the poor guy would have blood and guts all over his fancy apartment and expensive leather furnishings. No. I'd have to let him continue to believe I sold kitchen supplies until I could start my "real" job.

Luke and my brother, Scott, had been friends since the dawn of time, and of course, I'd had a crush on Luke almost as long. He'd been larger than life, larger than our dinky hometown and destined for greater things. After a stellar run as our school's most popular hockey player, Luke had gone off to university and then Stanford Law. The man was perfection—smart, beautiful... a mover and shaker who ran with the big dogs and wore four-thousand-dollar suits while getting martinis with multimillionaire legal clients. He dated the new Calvin Klein model whose gorgeous fucking face and even more gorgeous fucking body were plastered on billboards and magazines all over fucking town.

Not that I was bitter or jealous about it, because I fucking wasn't.

But the fact remained: there was no way in hell I was admitting to Luke Holland I sold nipple clamps for a living.

No fucking way.

When Sally dropped me off outside the apartment, I thanked her politely and dragged my sorry ass up to Luke's tenth-floor apartment. It was dark in the apartment except for a warm lamp glowing on one of the side tables by the couch. I assumed Luke was still out or already in his room for the night. After dropping my keys on the table by the door, I shrugged off my coat and set it with my messenger bag on the floor by the door.

My phone buzzed with a text.

Dante Marian: *Hi Noah, this is Dante from this afternoon at the vineyard. AJ and I have an extra ticket to a holiday a cappella concert next week and were hoping you might join us.*

I pumped my fist in the air like a fool. My first invitation to do something fun in my new city. I *knew* that family had been a bunch of sweethearts. I typed back immediately.

Noah Campbell: *I'd love to! Thank you so much for thinking of me. Just let me know where and when.*

Dante Marian: *Will do. Also, would it be okay if we set you up with someone for a double date? The guy's name is Jordan and he's the sweetest thing ever. He's a veterinarian at my mom's clinic.*

I thought about going on my first date in the city and felt the heady mix of nerves and excitement rattle through me.

Noah Campbell: *That would be great. Tell him I look forward to meeting him.*

After getting the details, I made my way to the kitchen area and rifled through the fridge for a bottle of water. With a giant grin on my face I gazed out at the twinkling lights of the city through the large windows on the other side of the dining table. Luke's apartment was an open floor plan with kitchen, dining, and living areas all one big space. There were huge windows on all sides showcasing the most magnificent views of the Bay Area. I felt lucky every time I caught a glimpse of my new city.

I sighed in contentment. Regardless of the reason for moving and the shitty job debacle, at least I was finally here. Finally on my own, chasing after what I wanted without all the interference of my family and my ex-boyfriend, Gordon. I'd spent too long listening to other people's advice about my own damned life, and now it was time to do what I wanted.

"Hey, how'd it go?" The deep, sexy voice sent shivers through me, and it was all I could do not to whimper. I turned around to see Luke standing behind me in the kitchen in nothing but a low-hanging pair of faded flannel pajama pants. His dark hair stuck up in tufts, and his beard scruff only added to the most gorgeous man face on the planet. As I stared at him, I couldn't help but focus on the sculpted chest and abs that were covered by a light smattering of dark hair that seriously taunted my tongue.

I gulped.

"Fine," I squeaked.

Well, *ahem*. That sucked. I cleared my throat and tried again. "Fine. It was fine."

Could I say fine one more time?

Luke's lip curved up at the corner. "Yes, Noah, but was it *fine*?"

He yawned and reached past me for the fridge door. I smelled the sleepy scent of him and decided maybe it would be better if I held my breath rather than sniff him and pop a boner. After grabbing his bottle of water, he looked at me funny.

"Come sit down and tell me all about it," he mumbled in a gruff voice.

"Were you asleep?" I asked. "I didn't mean to wake you."

He nodded, scratching his stomach sensually, like someone out of a porn video would. The only difference was he didn't seem to realize he was doing it. "I fell asleep as soon as I got home from the office and napped for a few hours. I'm going to be screwed getting to bed anytime soon."

I followed him into the living area and sat down on the opposite end of the couch, turning sideways until my back was against the arm and my leg was bent up beside me on the cushion so I could face him.

"I thought you had today off? Don't most people have a four-day weekend for American Thanksgiving?"

He smiled at me like I was naive. Just Scott's silly baby brother. "I don't take many days off, Noah. The law waits for no man."

"Ah, you're too important for rest and relaxation. I see."

Luke's face softened. "Not really. I'm just working on a really tough case right now and am trying to do my best for the client. Tell me how the first day on the new job went."

I felt my face heat up. "Oh. It was fi— I mean... yeah, good. The woman I work for is nice. The people at the event were really friendly and laid back. I liked them. It was weird being around so many gay couples at one time. I mean, I know that sounds strange," I admitted, looking down at my lap. "But you know what it's like back home. Even if people are cool with it, there just aren't a lot of couples our age. There were several gay couples at this party. I'm not used to that, you know? It was really sweet."

Luke's face opened into an understanding smile. "Yeah. I remember when I first moved here, noticing how many people were out and proud everywhere I went. It's so different. I guess I'm used to it now, and I forget. Did you guys sell lots of gadgets?"

I thought about the sheer number of sex acts that were going to be happening at the Alexander Vineyard tonight and shuddered. Once again, I gave a stern mental warning to my cock to be still. "Yes," I squeaked. "Yes, we sold lots of... gadgets."

Handcuffs and dildos and cock rings, oh my.

"Great, you'll have to bring home some samples of your stuff for us to try here in the apartment," he offered.

I pictured Luke trying the Magic Manhandler with the optional Titillator attachment, and my grip suddenly tightened on the end of my water bottle, causing it to jump out of my hands and tumble through the air three or four times until it landed on the floor several feet away and rolled to a stop at the base of the television cabinet. Silence descended between us.

"Haha," I said, standing up to retrieve it. "Good thing it was closed, right? Saved me from spurting everywhere. Or, ah, spilling... it, water. Oh god. I'll just... grab that."

As I bent over to grab the bottle I took the opportunity to sneak a peek at Luke to see if he was secretly laughing at me. For a minute I could have sworn I caught him staring at my ass. *Not everything and everyone is about sex, you jackass*, I thought. Clearly the sheer number of sexual innuendos and gestures I'd witnessed earlier that day had fried my brain. It was time for me to go to bed.

And maybe jack off. For research purposes. I was nothing if not diligent about putting my all into my new job.

I remembered Sally handing me samples of the holiday product line in preparation for the upcoming season, and I wondered if there was a Jack Frost in there. That thing would make my night a bit better. A little of the pumpkin-flavored lube wouldn't go amiss either. Maybe this job wasn't so bad after all. I turned to find my bag.

"Noah?" Luke asked.

"Huh?" I said, jumping around to face him again despite the giant hot patches on my cheeks.

"I'm glad it went well today. I know it's not easy moving to a new city, but I just want to make sure you know I'm here for you. If you need anything and can't get a hold of me, just ask my assistant Jasmine to get me, okay?"

My heart thudded in my chest at the gesture. I knew how busy and important he was at his firm, and I couldn't imagine ever taking him up on his offer to interrupt him at work. But the sentiment made me feel special nonetheless.

"Thanks, Luke. I really appreciate everything you've done to help me feel welcome. It's really generous of you," I said before heading toward my bedroom.

"No big deal," Luke said with a wink. "I promised Scott I'd keep you out of trouble. He'd kick my ass if I let anything happen to his baby brother."

Oh, right. Luke thought of me as Scott's baby brother. Of course he did. Why wouldn't he?

I wondered how long it would take me to shake off the reminder before I could successfully sample the Jack Frost to fantasies of Luke Holland stripping off those low-hanging pajama pants and taking me up against one of his large panoramic windows.

The toy wasn't even fully out of its box before I realized there was absolutely no need for it. Just the visual of Luke naked behind me, fucking into my body with the city lights spread out around us was enough to have me biting my pillow within minutes.

Maybe selling sex toys for a living wasn't a good idea when I hadn't gotten laid in six months. The more recent history of my relationship with my ex had included me servicing his needs and him being too tired to reciprocate. It was my turn. I wanted to fucking come without being the one to do all the work all the time.

I needed to meet someone. It was time to get out there. Here I was in San Francisco—an entire city of hot gay men at my disposal. Forget Gordon the Ex. Forget Luke the Crush. I'd put myself out there and meet someone new, someone sweet. They didn't need to become the next love of my life. I wasn't ready to enter into another relationship again anyway. But I sure as hell was ready to have some fun.

Dating had never been easy for someone as shy as I was, but as I fell asleep that night I decided to put myself out there and embrace new experiences. I needed to meet people in my new city, and my mom had always told me something she'd learned on Oprah long ago

—even if a blind date turned out to be wrong for you, he might lead you to Mr. Right, and in the process, he might just become your best friend.

2

LUKE

When I walked into work the following Monday morning, one of my law partners was waiting for me in my office. Pete was dressed in his usual power suit and had a mischievous glint in his eye.

"What's gotten into you? Or do I even want to know?" I asked, dropping my computer bag on the floor by my desk and slipping off my suit jacket.

"Hey, so, ah... Luke. I have someone I want to set you up with," he said.

"Hell no," I responded immediately. "Remember the last time you tried that? I went out with your brother, Blue, and he literally cried on my shoulder the entire night. Remember?"

Pete barked out a laugh. "That was a fluke. He'd just gotten dumped. That was my bad for arranging it too soon. I just felt sorry for the guy. He needed to know there were better men out there than that asshole Jeremy."

"Then there was the night you forced me to go with you to Harry Dick's to check out Griff's new boyfriend, and I inadvertently wound up being the meat in a twin sandwich on the dance floor."

Pete raised an eyebrow at me. "And that was a bad thing? You're complaining?"

I thought about how many hands were on my body that night. "No. Come to think of it. That was a bad example."

"Right. So, my ideas aren't all that bad. Give me a chance. Ginger agrees this guy would be perfect for you. He's sweet and eager. Might actually tame the tiger in you, Luke."

I rolled my eyes. "I need sweet and eager like a hole in the head. It'd be lower maintenance to just get a puppy."

"What kind of guy are you looking for, then?" he asked, sitting back in the chair across the desk from me.

I couldn't help but think of Scott's brother, Noah. The kid whose face and body I'd spent the entire weekend jacking off to in my room. I felt my cheeks heat up. "I'm not looking," I said, truthfully. "Things are too busy here at the firm. You of all people should know that. Plus, in case you forgot, I have Victor."

"You need to ditch that fucker."

He was right, but I wasn't about to let him know that. "Why in the world would I ditch a cover model who sucks cock like a—"

Pete held up a hand. "I get it. No need to continue. I heard enough sex talk from my brothers this weekend to satisfy me for a while. If I never hear the word cock again as long as I live, it'll be too soon. They even made me sit through a dildo demonstration."

"Again?" I asked with a laugh. "I need to become friends with your brothers. They have the best parties."

"Yes, again. Dante and AJ got engaged and had that sex toy lady come. Actually, that's how I met the guy I want to set you up with. He works with her."

I studied Pete, wondering if he was being serious or just pulling my leg as usual. "You want to set me up with some weirdo who sells Love Junk?"

"He's sweet, Luke. I have a feeling about this guy," Pete said sincerely. "He'd be good for you."

The sentiment was touching. Pete and I had been friends and business partners for years, but he'd never interfered in my love life. "I'll think about it, okay? But right now I need to focus on the Samari case. Are you going to be in the deposition later this morning?"

We changed our focus to the work of the day, but I couldn't help imagining what it would be like to date a guy who knew all the ins and outs of sex toys. That would probably be kind of fun.

IT WAS ALMOST ten when I arrived home that night. I'd worked late before I met Victor and some of his friends for a drink and a bite to eat. They'd spent the entire time trashing a fellow model who'd had the audacity to turn down a photo shoot with someone called Sartorio in order to walk in his own college graduation ceremony. By the time I'd finished dinner, I was over it.

Victor had asked to come back to my place, sliding his slender hand seductively up my thigh, purposefully waking up my sleeping dick. I'd agreed with his self-serving invitation and paid the check before grabbing his hand and leading him out of there.

Once in the elevator to my apartment, Victor pounced. His lips attacked mine while his hands began fumbling with my belt.

"Not here, Jesus," I muttered against his mouth. "I have a room-mate now, remember? Don't want my dick hanging out when I walk into the apartment."

"I'll hide it in my mouth. How about that?" Victor teased. The elevator door opened and we stepped out, Victor's hands never letting go of my belt buckle.

When I opened the apartment door, he jumped me again before I even had a chance to get the door closed behind us. "I've been thinking about your cock all day," he said against my neck. "That fat cock filling me up. Pounding me into the bed, the floor, whatever the fuck." His hands were wrapped tightly around my neck and he'd crawled up my body until his thin legs were wrapped around my waist. He was skin and bones from starving himself for his last photo shoot.

I managed to begin the walk to my bedroom with his slim form wrapped around my waist when I heard the crash of glass from the direction of the kitchen. Victor ignored it and kept whispering dirty words in my ear as if nothing had happened. I peeled him off me before turning to investigate.

There, in the dim light of the single bulb over the stove, I saw Noah standing over a broken flower vase in a T-shirt and pajama pants. His light brown hair stood up in the back like he'd been lying on it funny and his eyebrows were creased with worry. He was even more adorable than usual. For some reason I'd always found myself wanting to grab him up in a hug like I was his grandmother or something. Tonight, I realized the feeling had gotten stronger since he'd moved in with me. I shook my head to rid it of those ridiculous thoughts.

"You okay?" I asked. "You're barefooted. Stay right there."

Noah's head jerked up in surprise and his lips fell open. "Sorry... I-I, ah, broke a vase. But don't worry, it wasn't one of yours."

He stared down at the mess in frustration before looking back up at me with a look on his face I couldn't quite decipher.

Slivers of glass shined in the dim light all over the kitchen floor. The last thing I wanted was for him to move his feet and wind up with a nasty cut. I carefully stepped through the wreckage in my dress shoes and reached around Noah's waist to lift him out of the danger zone. As soon as my arms went around him, he sucked in a breath and clutched my shoulders to keep from falling.

"What're you doing?" he blurted. His breath smelled faintly of mint, and I wondered if he'd already brushed his teeth and gotten ready for bed even though it wasn't ten p.m. yet.

"Moving you to safety. I don't want you to cut yourself," I said, trying desperately not to sniff him. He must have taken a shower recently because he smelled like the sandalwood soap I'd put in his bathroom before he'd arrived the week before. I moved him several feet away to the dining area before walking toward the pantry closet to find a broom.

"You don't need to clean that up," he said. "Let me just grab some shoes." He turned to go toward his bedroom, but I stopped him.

"It'll be done by the time you get back. Stay there." I carefully picked up the larger pieces and deposited them into an empty cereal box I pulled out of the recycling bin. I noticed a clump of fresh flowers among the shattered glass. "These are pretty. Did you pick them up this afternoon?" I asked while I set them aside carefully to rinse in the sink.

"No, ah..." he stammered. I looked up at him, noticing the adorable pink flush spread across his cheeks.

"Noah?" I teased. I noticed Noah tug at the hem of his T-shirt self-consciously. It was soft and faded red with BAZINGA written across it in superhero font. That's when I noticed his light blue pajama pants were covered in a repeat pattern of little curled-up kitty cats. The man was the cutest fucking thing ever.

"No. Ah..." he repeated accidentally before blushing even deeper and laughing at himself. "I mean, no, someone sent them to me."

I felt my smile falter just a bit.

"Babe?" Victor's voice came from behind me. "You coming to bed?"

I turned around to face him, having forgotten I'd brought Victor home with me. "Just a sec," I told him before turning back to Noah while I swept up some of the shards of glass. "Who sent you the flowers? Your ex?" It was really none of my business, but I wanted to know. I remembered Scott telling me Noah's ex was a close family friend of theirs.

His eyes darted around before landing on his feet. "No, not Gord. Just this guy. I don't know him really. We have a date later this week. It's like a setup thing."

An uneasy feeling jangled in my stomach. "A setup? With whom? A stranger? Don't you think that's dangerous?"

Noah's face came up to look at me. "His name is Jordan. It's a double date with one of the couples I met last Friday. You know, when I did that sales event for work? They're setting me up with a friend of theirs, and he sent flowers to tell me how much he was looking forward to meeting me."

What a presumptuous douche, I thought. "That's great," I said, trying to force a smile.

"We'll see. Anyway, I was trying to add water since it came with an empty vase. That's when I heard a noise. I must have jumped. Next thing I know, the vase is on the floor."

"Sorry. I should have said something. It was dark so I thought you weren't around." I finished cleaning up the last of the glass before looking back up at him. Noah studied me again. He seemed to do that a lot lately.

"It's okay. I didn't realize you had company. Please let me finish cleaning up so you can go back to him," he said in a soft voice.

I looked back over my shoulder to where Victor appeared to be picking lint off his shirt. "What? It's just Victor. He's not company."

Noah blew out a breath and reached for the broom. "Fine, I didn't realize you had your *boyfriend* here. Now give me that."

I wanted to tell him Victor wasn't my boyfriend, but I also didn't want to sound crass. *He's just someone I fuck regularly*, didn't quite sound right. Made me feel like a user. Which I most certainly wasn't. Victor and I had always been on the same page about what we had, what we wanted. Both of us had all-consuming careers with no room for the emotional crap that came with relationships.

But I didn't correct Noah. I wasn't even sure why, exactly. Was it because I didn't want him to think less of me? And if so, why? What did it matter? It didn't. Why was I even wasting my time worrying about what Scott's little brother thought? I needed to remember I had a hot underwear model waiting for me to bend him over my bed.

I handed over the broom without another word before turning back to Victor.

"Let's go."

3

NOAH

Why were my hands shaking? I'd been on dates before, even blind dates. So why the hell was I so nervous? Honestly, I blamed Luke. He'd been all up in my face the entire time I'd tried to get ready for the date. I didn't even know why he was home so early.

"Remind me again why you're even here?" I asked as I flipped through shirts in my closet in search of something better than what I actually owned. "I don't usually see you before seven thirty on a work night."

Luke was sitting on my bed with his back to the headboard, his shoes, suit jacket, and tie missing but the rest was the perfect image of the put-together attorney. His long fingers fiddled with the corner of one of the throw pillows my mother had insisted on buying me to make my room appear "homier."

"I had a meeting across town, and it finished early. There was no reason to go all the way back to the office so late in the day. I can work from here on my laptop."

I pulled out a button-down shirt with tiny atoms printed on it. They were so small, the shirt could pass for any old printed button-down, but I loved wearing it, knowing it was unique.

I pursed my lips before putting it back in the closet.

"What was wrong with that one?" Luke asked.

"Too geeky," I responded before pulling out a solid red shirt. "I should go for something more standard."

"More boring, you mean?"

"Less likely to make someone think I'm weird," I corrected.

"But you *are* weird," he teased. "Might as well get that out of the way early and give the poor guy a chance to bolt from the get-go."

I picked up a ball cap from a low shelf and flung it at his head. "Nice, jackass. You're not helping."

Luke ducked and reached out to catch the cap, sliding it easily onto his head. God, the sight of my cap on his head did things to me. I looked away.

"What about this one?" I asked, pulling out a white shirt with red and green stripes. "Kind of seasonal, right?"

"Wear the first one. It suits you." Luke's voice sounded funny so I turned to look at him. His eyes were locked on mine. "It's your favorite, Noah. So wear it. If you feel good in what you're wearing, you'll be more relaxed and confident, and the guy will have a better chance at seeing the real you." Luke slid off my bed and headed for the door to my room.

"How do you know it's my favorite?" I called after him.

There was no response.

I picked the one he suggested in hopes he was right. I needed all the confidence I could get.

By the time the doorbell rang, I was so nervous the nausea had set in. I wondered if it was because Gordon and I had been together so long I'd forgotten how to do the whole dating thing, or if maybe it was the nerves of being in a strange town without the usual famil-iarity of my surroundings. I stopped pacing in the living room and glanced over at Luke who seemed to be watching me.

"I'll get it," he said, moving toward the door.

"Stop!" I blurted. He slowly turned on his heel to stare at me like I was insane. Which I pretty much was. "Ah, I mean... I'll get it. I wouldn't want you to have to..."

"What's the problem, Noah?"

I blew out a huffy breath, feeling like a brat, but I decided to tell him the truth anyway for the sake of time. "It's just... if he sees you first, he's not going to want to go out with me, okay?"

There, I'd said it.

Luke's eyebrows raised to the ceiling. "What? Are you crazy?"

"Shut up, you're gorgeous. I'm a skinny awkward geek. Give me a fighting chance with this guy, please?" I asked. I felt the embarrassment bloom hot in my cheeks.

Luke's face changed from confusion to something too close to pity for my liking. I flapped my hand at him. "Plus, I don't need a grumpy, overprotective brother there for this either," I grumbled.

He didn't say another word, just turned to head back to his bedroom.

I let out a breath as the doorbell rang again.

It was time.

~

THE DATE WAS for a holiday a cappella concert, followed by a late dinner at a nice Italian restaurant. The guy I'd been set up with was exactly the way Dante had described him—a total sweetheart. He'd greeted me with a friendly smile and kiss on the cheek and continued to use gentlemanly manners all evening like opening doors for me and putting his hand on my lower back when we were in crowded areas like the lobby of the concert hall.

By the time we made it to the restaurant after the concert, I felt much more relaxed in his presence. I'd also remembered how nice Dante and AJ were. They made every point to include me in the conversations and get to know me. After placing our dinner orders, Jordan nudged my shoulder with his own in the dark corner booth where we sat.

"So, Nate, Dante and AJ tell me you're from Canada. What made you decide to move to the States?" Jordan asked with a smile. Dante and AJ sat across from us in the booth, AJ's arm settled comfortably behind his fiancé's shoulders, his fingers sneaking up into Dante's hair. If Dante had been a cat, he'd have been purring.

"It's Noah, actually," I said for at least the second time that night. I was pretty sure I caught AJ wince out of the corner of my eye. "Ah, let's see, I lived in a very, very small town. I'd always wanted to move to a big city like this, but I guess it took a while before I finally pulled the trigger. What about you? Are you from here originally?"

Jordan leaned back into the booth, pulling his drink glass with him and taking a sip from his cocktail. "I'm from a little farm town in Missouri, actually. I came to California for vet school, thinking I'd become a large animal vet and go back home to practice. But I fell in love with the city. And when I thought about how hard it would be to meet other gay men back home, it kind of made the decision to stay easier." He shot me a flirty wink and moved a little closer in the booth to me until our thighs brushed together.

"What about you two?" I asked, looking across to Dante and AJ. "You guys from the Bay Area too?"

"No, but we're here for good now." AJ answered for the both of them while Dante smiled up at him. "Most of Dante's family is here, and mine are scattered all over. We want to live near family. Plus, Dante runs a gay youth shelter here in town. Everyone there is like our family too."

"Really? I'd love to hear more about it. Does the shelter need volunteers?" I felt my face flush with embarrassment as I realized that was probably a silly question.

Dante's face lit up. "Of course we do. Always. We'd love to have you, Noah. And it'll be a great way to meet new people here in town too."

"Excellent. I did some volunteer work back home, but of course we didn't have a gay youth shelter there. Mostly a food bank and things like that," I said before turning to Jordan. "Do you volunteer there, too?"

He chuckled. "No. Not yet, anyway. Maybe I'll join you though. Been meaning to check it out. Everyone at the clinic where I work is involved in the shelter in some form or another."

As the food was served, the conversation remained comfortable if not particularly riveting. I enjoyed watching Dante and AJ flirt and whisper to each other throughout the meal. AJ seemed like the most attentive boyfriend I'd ever seen, always offering things like the salt and pepper to Dante before using them himself. At one point while AJ told us about a movie they'd seen the weekend before, Dante accidentally dropped his fork under the table and AJ handed his over without skipping a beat. Dante simply leaned over and dropped a kiss of thanks on AJ's cheek before digging back into his pasta.

It took me until dessert to realize I was considerably more attracted to the relationship in front of me than the man sitting next to me.

I knew it wasn't something that happened on any first date. Surely even Dante and AJ hadn't forged their magical connection in the very first night of their acquaintance, so I put more effort into getting to know Jordan. I asked him about his work, his family, his interests outside of work. He seemed to thrive on the attention and shared more and more of himself with me before finally realizing he was monopolizing the conversation.

"Why am I going on and on about myself?" he asked with a roll of his eyes. "I'm so sorry. What about you, Noah? Any hobbies? I haven't even asked what you do for a living. Dante just said he met you through your job."

In my mind, I heard the screech of brakes and the inevitable crunch of fenders. *Abort, abort,* I thought. How the hell was I supposed to tell this veterinarian I sold a product called Buttjuice?

I glanced at Dante and AJ, whose matching soft smiles of support made me feel warm inside. "Ah, I'm in... direct sales," I said.

"Really? What do you sell?" Jordan asked, setting down his fork, wiping the napkin over his mouth, and sitting back in the booth with an arm stretched behind me.

Another quick glance across from me showed AJ hiding a grin under his napkin. Okay, so maybe there was a limit to their support.

I gulped. "Well, it's kind of a funny story."

~

IT TURNS out that telling a guy you sell sex toys for a living is like slathering yourself in a vat of Buttjuice and crooking a finger at the guy while shooting him fuck-me eyes. The rest of the date was spent surreptitiously fending off his advances under the table. I'd been so shocked the first time his hand had landed on my upper thigh, I'd jumped and knocked over a water glass.

When Jordan had asked Dante and AJ to stay in the car while he walked me up to my apartment, I'd tried giving huge scaredy-cat eyes to Dante. Unfortunately, he was too busy giving fuck-me eyes to AJ, and it was a lost cause.

Before getting my door unlocked, the guy was on me, pushing me up against the apartment door and kissing me. Jordan's lips landed on mine with a groan and a grunt while his hands began to feel me up all over.

"God, Noah, I've been wanting to touch you all night. So fucking sexy," he said into my mouth. His tongue fought its way down my throat. I could taste his dinner, and I had to restrain myself from gagging.

"Stop, stop," I said, pushing at his chest. It was too much, too fast for me. But just before opening my mouth to tell him to slow down, the apartment door opened and I fell backward onto my ass, rolling all the way over until I was facing forward on my knees again like I'd done some kind of gymnastics stunt. *What the hell?*

"Get the fuck out!" a familiar voice barked.

"Luke?" I asked, confused.

He stood in the doorway, somehow between Jordan and me.

"He said stop, you asshole. When a guy says stop, you *stop*," he growled.

I'd never heard Luke Holland lose his temper like that.

"Now get the fuck out and never call him again."

"W-wait a second," Jordan stammered. "Who the hell are you?"

Luke turned around and stepped past me, rushing to grab the flowers where they sat in a new vase on the kitchen counter. He plucked them out of the vase and carried the dripping stems over to where Jordan still stood gawping in the hallway.

"I'm his big brother, and you can take these with you," Luke spat before slamming the door in his face and locking it.

I was still on my knees in complete shock.

Luke's breath still heaved when he turned to face me and squatted down in front of me. "Are you okay?" he asked in a soft voice.

"Um, yeah? What the hell just happened, Luke?"

He looked at me like I was an idiot. "What just happened was I stopped him from attacking you."

"But Luke, he was just kissing me good night," I told him.

His eyes widened. "Are you saying you wanted it? You liked what he was doing to you?"

I felt my cheeks heat and looked down at where my hands rested on my thighs. "Well, no. It was a little aggressive, but I was about to tell him that myself."

Luke's jaw tightened. "Now you don't have to. I did it for you." He stood up and muttered under his breath, "Fucking asshole," before reaching a hand out to help me up.

"How did you even know we were out there?" I asked, still confused by what had happened. "It's after midnight; I thought you'd be asleep."

"I couldn't get to sleep. I was walking past the door to get a drink from the kitchen when I heard you say stop. I freaked out. Thought someone was hurting you."

His jaw clenched as he made his way into the kitchen. I trailed behind him to get a glass of water.

"I'm sorry. He wasn't hurting me. Just being very forward," I said, trying to assure him I was okay. "But thank you anyway. At least you saved me from having to turn down his next offer of a date."

I smiled at him, intending it as a joke but he looked confused. "What do you mean?"

"I'm pretty sure he's never going to ask me out again after meeting my 'big brother,'" I said, putting the term in finger quotes.

Luke had the grace to look sheepish. "Yeah, sorry about that. I might have overreacted. It's just... it's hard not to be protective of you, you know?"

"Why?" I asked, even though I shouldn't have.

"You're Scott's broth—"

I lunged forward to clamp a hand over his mouth without thinking. "Don't!"

His eyes widened until the gorgeous dark blue irises were surrounded by white on all sides.

We stood there frozen, eyes locked together in shock at my actions. His warm breath streamed over my knuckles in a soft caress. His breathing stretched the thin cotton of an old undershirt over his broad chest, and I realized we stood only inches apart.

Luke Holland was fucking magnificent. Tall and dark-haired. Muscled and fit. Face prickly with beard scruff after a long day at the office. He smelled like goose-down pillows and some kind of lemon scent, mixed in with the mint of toothpaste. He'd been in bed.

I couldn't help but picture Luke there, nestled in his covers and all warm and sleepy and relaxed. I felt my cock do the opposite. It woke up and roared to life—fucking *roared* to life. So much so that I had to get out of there before Luke saw my humiliating reaction to touching him.

"Sorry," I squeaked before turning to bolt to my room.

"Noah, wait!" Luke called out.

But there was no way in hell I was turning back.

4

LUKE

I stared after Noah in shock. What had just happened? One minute we'd been bickering about me prematurely saving him from that asshole, and the next I felt like his hand on my mouth might as well have been on my dick.

He'd been standing so close to me all I could see were the plump red lips still moist with some other man's saliva. The feeling infuriated me. I had a completely irrational anger toward the fucker in the hallway. What the hell had he been thinking coming on so strong to a kid?

Noah's not a kid anymore.

The voice in my head was the devil, and I tried so hard to ignore it.

It was a good thing Noah hadn't turned back after he'd walked away from me, or he would have seen the giant tent in my lounge pants. I looked down at my stupid cock. Stupid, stupid cock.

Since when do you get hard for Scott's baby brother? Jesus fuck. You've known him since he was practically a fetus.

I blew out a breath and opened the refrigerator door, standing in front of the open fridge to let the interior air cool me down despite the fact it was December. Maybe it was a hot flash. Did guys get those too? Maybe it was hormonal.

It was definitely hormonal.

Maybe it was a premature midlife crisis. Was that a thing?

I grabbed the bottle of water I'd been looking for and returned to my bedroom, unable to stop obsessing about the tingling sensation I still felt on my face from where Noah's palm had covered it.

His hand had felt warm and strong. It had smelled of buttered popcorn, and I realized he must have been wearing the same gloves he'd worn to the movies with me the night before. I'd gotten home late from work that night and noticed him slipping his coat on to go out.

"Where are you off to?" I'd asked.

"There's an old theater down the street that's playing some Doris Day movies," he'd said with an adorable pink blush on his skin. "I thought I'd go check it out."

"By yourself?"

He'd stood up straighter and jutted his chin out a little. "Yes. By myself. Why? Did you want to join me?"

I'd had at least two hours left of work I needed to do on the case I was working on, but for some reason I'd said yes.

We'd sat through two movies and shared a big tub of buttered popcorn. Several times I'd looked over and noticed how much he'd been enjoying himself. I knew there'd been nothing even close to this experience in our hometown, and I'd been secretly glad I'd been there to see him take advantage of one of the perks of his new city.

On the walk home through the cold night, he'd chatted animatedly about one of the movies.

"And the best friend shoving that food through the lunch counter holes in the wall like a life-sized vending machine. Wasn't that weird? I've always wondered if it was really like that back then. And then Cary Grant's best friend shows up and the lunch lady thinks he's the one who's been messing with Doris Day..." he kept explaining the parts he'd found funny, occasionally interrupting himself with a case of the giggles. "God, I love that movie. *A Touch of Mink*. Had you ever seen it?"

I shook my head and smiled at him, enjoying seeing him fully relaxed and happy. "No, but it was really good. I'm glad I went."

We'd gotten home and gone our separate ways into our bedrooms. It had been well into the wee hours of the morning, but I'd still been unable to get to sleep. Every time I'd begun to drift off, I'd imagined Noah's face bright with laughter, cheeks pink from the cold night air and wisps of hair peeking out from his warm wool hat. Every time that image had flashed into my half-asleep head, I'd gone hard and sat up gasping in surprise. Then I'd have to talk myself out of the roommate boner before trying to sleep again, only to come fully awake again not twenty minutes later with the same image burned into my brain and the same hard cock banging around in my boxer briefs.

It had finally taken some lube and a quick few strokes to put myself out of my misery and get to sleep. I'd put the entire unsettling experience out of my head until tonight. Until feeling Noah's warm hand on my face and smelling that buttered popcorn scent.

What the hell was I doing allowing myself to get turned on by Noah Campbell?

I lay back down in bed, unable to get the feel of his handprint off my skin. And if I had to jack off again that night to the memory of how close his full lips had been to my face, at least I could console myself with the fact my best friend Scott couldn't read minds.

The next morning when I entered the conference room to prepare for another in an endless string of depositions, I saw Pete.

"Good morning, sunshine. What's with the raccoon eyes?" Pete asked, popping a coffee pod into the machine on a side table.

"Trouble sleeping. It's fine. We all set for Mrs. Lorenzo? I have my list of questions, but feel free to add to it if you think of something."

"Yeah, we're good. Why are you having trouble sleeping? I'm falling into bed every night like an anvil. Ginger's pissed because I haven't touched her in weeks. I'm not even sure I'd know what to do with her if she got naked," he said with a laugh. "This case is killing me."

"TMI, Pete, Jesus."

"Seriously, Luke. Is something on your mind? Tell Uncle Petey all about it." His grin was teasing, but I knew he meant it. He'd always been a good listener and an even better friend.

"I'm having inappropriate thoughts about my best friend's little brother," I admitted. "And he's living with me, so it's like ten times worse than it would be if he was... oh... say, back in Canada."

"Define little," Pete said. "You're thirty-five, Luke. Just how young is this kid?"

"No, Jesus. It's not that. He's twenty-eight. It's just... he's always been Scott's kid brother, you know? Tagging along, annoying the shit out of us. A kid."

"Are you saying you want to sleep with him?"

I glared at him. "What? No! Of course not."

Lie. *Total* lie.

"It's just..." I blew out a breath. "I don't know why I'm having these thoughts now, all of a sudden. He's just a regular guy, you know? Nothing special. And I'm sleeping with an underwear model, for god's sake."

For some reason, saying Noah was nothing special felt more like a lie than claiming I didn't want to sleep with him. Of course he was special. He was smart and funny and—

"Were you ever attracted to his brother?" Pete asked.

"Scott? Ew, gross. No. Hell no. Gross."

Pete laughed and held up his hands. "Okay, okay. Well, why don't you ask him out? You make it sound like things aren't serious with Victor, so why not give it a try with this kid?"

"No. That would seriously complicate things. First of all, he's Scott's brother—practically my own brother. Secondly, he's my roommate. Third of all, I'm perfectly happy with Victor. Well, I mean... maybe not that last part. He's a bit of an airhead if you want to know the truth."

"A bit?" Pete eyed me with a smirk. "Try a ginormous airhead. My brother Blue said he saw an interview with him where Victor insisted Poland was at the North Pole."

I snorted. "Shut up. I get your point. Maybe I need to find someone new."

"Maybe it's time for you to find someone to fall in love with instead of fuck," Pete suggested, finally taking a seat at the table next to me. "Which works out great for me because I promised Ginger I'd find a date for this guy she wants to set up. The one I mentioned to you."

"Hell no, Pete. No. I already told you—no blind date with some weirdo," I said. "You're fucking nuts if you think I'm letting you guys set me up. Last time I let *Ginger* set me up, I ended up at the guy's parents' house for family dinner."

"Shut the fuck up. That was a mistake and you know it. Had I known she was going to set you up with my brother Maverick, I would have stopped it. And you love my family. You've been to family dinner a million times."

"Not as an actual member of the family. I thought poor Maverick was going to faint," I said with a laugh. "Too bad things didn't work out between us. We might have been able to keep him in California if they had."

"He's happily married, living in South Carolina. His vet practice is thriving, and Beau's contracting business is massive after the hurricane rebuilding. I think they're right where they're supposed to be," Pete said with a smile. "Of course, Mom keeps asking when they're going to start a family now that they're so settled."

"Seven grandkids isn't enough for Rebecca? Maybe you and Ginger should—"

"Shut your fucking mouth," Pete blurted. "Don't even put that out into the universe. I believe we have our hands full enough as it is, thank you very much."

"You're only saying that because Tommy is in his terrible twos. Once he's seven like the girls were when he was born, you'll get the itch again," I teased.

"I will fuck you up, Luke. Don't think I won't," he growled. "Just for that, the blind date isn't optional. You're taking this guy to the office holiday party."

I blinked at him in surprise. "What? No, I most certainly am not. Are you crazy?"

"No, not crazy. Just determined. When Ginger puts her mind to something, my life is hell until she gets it. So you will do this for me because you love me."

"I don't."

Pete batted his eyelashes. "You do. Plus, he's a cute guy. You should have seen the way all of my brothers and their spouses drooled over him when they met him."

"Really?"

"Yes."

"Wow. He must be something, then. Maybe I'll take you up on your offer after all," I said. "But why the firm's holiday party? Don't you think that will be a little awkward for the guy? He won't know anyone."

"That's part of the reason Ginger wants to do it that way. He can meet plenty of other people in case he doesn't like you and wants to trade you out for someone else."

I flicked his shoulder with my fingers. "Nice."

Pete laughed and opened his laptop. "Honestly, I think she just didn't want to have to listen to Victor explain the difference between a thong and a jockstrap one more time."

"That was one time, jackass. And you'd be surprised how often people confuse the—oh, never mind. As long as he's not an *actual* Marian this time, I'll give it a try. Better than trying to explain to Victor again that *lawyer* and *attorney* aren't two different levels of management at the firm. I think he equates them to private and general or something. Legal ranks instead of military ranks." I rolled my eyes and got to work as Pete kept laughing.

The rest of Friday went by in a flash with depositions, a client lunch meeting, strategy meetings, and a bar association happy hour after work. While at the bar, I got a call from my aunt back in Alberta.

I stood and put down some cash before stepping out to take the call on the sidewalk.

"Hi, Aunt Sandy," I said once I was able to hear her.

"Lucas, there you are." Her voice was light and comforting. After my mom passed away when I was eighteen, Sandy had become the closest thing I had to a mother. Even though I never truly lived with Sandy and Dalton, they remained my home base. I knew right off Aunt Sandy was calling to make sure I'd made my reservations to visit for Christmas.

"I emailed Uncle Dalton my plane reservations," I said, trying to prevent her from asking.

"Yes, dear. He printed them out and put them on the calendar. That's fine. I was, ah..." Her voice trailed off as if she was trying to find the words to ask me something difficult.

"Is everything alright?"

"Oh, yes. Fine. Of course. It's just that... well, I was curious if maybe you'd like to bring..." I heard my uncle's muffled voice in the background before Sandy spoke again. "We wanted to know if there was someone special you'd like to bring home for the holidays, dear."

I felt my cheeks stretch into a smile. Lord only knew how long it had taken her to get up the nerve to ask me that. Sandy and Dalton had always known I was gay, but they'd never really acknowledged it. It wasn't that they were homophobic; it was more that they were unsure of how to approach talking about it. It was so foreign to them, they'd often say things in an awkward, gender-neutral manner.

"Luke?" Sandy asked when I hesitated a minute too long.

"No, Aunt Sandy. No one special enough to bring home this year," I said. "But thank you for offering. That's very nice of you."

There was a moment of silence before her voice came back on, softer than before. "Lucas, honey, we worry about you. When are you going to meet someone and settle down?"

For some reason, the image of Noah cuddled up under a blanket on my sofa flashed before my eyes. I blew out a breath and rubbed a temple with the fingers of my free hand.

"I'm not really the settling down type, Aunt Sandy," I said. "I'm married to my job."

The lame excuse felt like exactly that when it escaped my lips.

"Nonsense," she scoffed. "You just haven't met the right person. Once you do, you'll see there are more important things out there than lawsuits."

I thought about the string of boyfriends my mom had after my dad died. How I'd gotten attached to each one and then never seen them again when she'd gotten tired of them.

"Relationships don't work out all the time, Sandy," I confessed. "I think it's easier for me to just date around and keep things light, you know?"

Another moment of silence.

"You're not your mother, Lucas Holland," she admonished. "I wish to god you could have seen your parents together. Then you'd know love is worth it."

I felt my teeth clack together at the familiar sentiment. "If they had it Sandy... well, a fat lot of good it did either one of them in the end."

Her sigh was resigned. "Promise me you'll look out for yourself down there, Luke. I'd feel better if you'd at least agree to go on a couple of dates for my sake."

I barked out a laugh, causing a young woman on the sidewalk to jump and glare at me. After flashing her a nod of apology, I returned to my call. "I'll be sure to mention to the next cute guy I see that my auntie would like me to ask him out on a proper date."

Sandy chuckled. "You do that, Lucas. Promise me."

I thought about Pete's offer to set me up. What would it hurt to accept one date?

"I promise."

By the time I got home, I was too tired to even check on Noah. I went straight to my room and fell into a dreamless sleep.

5

NOAH

Later that week, Dante and AJ invited me to join their family for a game night at his parents' house in Hillsborough. He'd said it was something his family tried to do more of around the holidays and it usually entailed lots of competition, yelling, posturing, and obnoxious teasing in addition to plenty of food and drink. Sounded like the kind of spectacle I'd enjoy witnessing.

When my ride pulled up in front of the sprawling mid-century modern home that Saturday night, I was taken aback by the realization that the Marian family must be loaded. Sally had told me at the first sales party we did that one of the brothers owned the vineyard with his husband, but I hadn't realized the entire family was that wealthy too. I looked down at my simple red henley shirt and blue jeans. I hoped I wasn't underdressed.

"You're here!"

My head snapped up to see a familiar face standing in the doorway with a big grin. "Simone, right?" I asked. "Dante's sister?"

"You got it. Come on in and see everyone. Let me take your coat," she said.

When I entered the house, I immediately heard the buzz of several people talking over each other. Holiday music played in the background, but it was practically impossible to hear over all the voices and laughter.

I followed Simone into a huge kitchen and saw gorgeous Marian men as far as the eye could see. For just a moment, I was struck with a sense of bad timing—maybe if I'd just moved to the area a few years earlier, I would have stood a chance at getting one of those beautiful men to go out with me. But it was clear from the sheer number of hands on asses that they were all happily matched.

"Everyone, you remember Noah. Noah, this is everyone," Simone called out. "What do you want to drink?"

After getting settled in the large family room with a glass of wine, I realized it was much easier to get to know everyone than I'd antici- pated. They were a friendly crew. Every time I found myself with no one to talk to, someone would notice and quickly remedy the situation.

"So, Noah, how did you end up selling Love Junk?" Teddy asked with a mischievous glint in his eyes. "Was it for the employee discount?" I felt my face heat up.

"Um, yeah, so, about that..." Everyone chuckled as I took a deep breath. "I didn't really know what I was getting myself into. I guess you could say I was desperate to take anything I could get. I'd broken up with my boyfriend and—"

Simone cut me off. "Why?"

"Huh?"

"Why did you two break if off?"

"Nosy bitch," her brother Blue murmured under his breath. She smacked him in the stomach, causing an *oof* to come out. Fortunately, Blue's husband, Tristan, was there to soothe him with a kiss. I couldn't help but stare. They were both very good-looking men, but more than that, they were sweet and loving in a way I hadn't really seen before.

Jude reached over and squeezed my arm gently. "You were saying?"

I took another second to wonder at the incredible turn my life had taken. In less than two short weeks, I'd gone from being a nobody nurse in a tiny town in Alberta to being a sex toy slinger in Gay Mecca, USA.

"Why did I break it off with Gordon? Well, it's kind of embarrassing, really." I looked around at the room full of mostly gay men. Understanding and supportive looks warmed all their faces. "He's a fighter pilot stationed at Four Wing, which is in my hometown of Cold Lake. His sister is, ah, married to my brother. We met through them and started dating in university but broke up when he dropped out to enlist in the air force. Once he was stationed back home, we reconnected. I was a nurse at the local hospital, and after we started dating again, he just sort of... moved in, I guess. He said it was nicer staying with me than staying on base. The next thing I knew, it had been three or four years, and I was settling for a life I'd never wanted. I didn't realize I'd become Gord's glorified domestic servant—cooking, cleaning, pressing his uniforms, hosting poker nights for him and his buddies. It wasn't until I overheard him making some nasty comments about it to his friends in a bar one night that I'd realized I'd just let it all happen. Time passes whether you're paying attention or not, you know? Sometimes you just have to wake the hell up and make stuff happen for yourself regardless of what anyone else thinks."

Jude squeezed my arm again. "Yeah," he said quietly. "Ain't that the truth." I caught him locking eyes with his husband, Derek, across the room. The small smile on Derek's face indicated some kind of meaning between the two of them that I couldn't deduce.

Teddy sighed from his spot on the floor next to his husband, Jamie. "I couldn't agree more. If you want something, you have to go for it. No sense in having half of what you want if the other half is thousands of miles away, right, sweetheart?" He rested his hand on Jamie's jean-clad thigh next to him, and Jamie leaned in to Teddy's shoulder.

"Right. It's not always easy, though. I'm proud of you, Noah. I'm sure the decision wasn't painless," Jamie said with an understanding tone.

"No," I said with a laugh. "That's for sure. It was one of the hardest things I've ever done."

Tristan took a sip of his beer and leaned forward. "How did Gordon take the news when you broke it off?"

The laughter died on my lips as I felt the familiar stutter-step of my heart at the thought of Gord coming home to an empty apartment.

"Dunno," I admitted. "I chickened out and left while he was away on a training flight."

I tried not to think about the ripple effect of my sudden departure on my sister-in-law, Rose. Or the rest of our families, for that matter. I was fairly sure Gordon and Rose's parents would be thrilled. No more gay relationship to embarrass them around town.

Simone sucked in a noisy breath. "You're shitting me. Just left with no warning? Whoa."

"Man, that takes balls," AJ muttered before tossing a handful of candied almonds into his mouth.

There was a commotion by the door to the large family room, and I noticed a few more guys entering.

"What takes balls, brother?" a man with curly hair and a goofy smile asked, plunking down a six-pack of beer on the big, heavy wooden coffee table. I couldn't remember the man's name from the vineyard party, but I knew the brown-haired man next to him was his partner.

"Hey, Griff!" Dante said, eyes lighting up as he stood to hug his older brother. "Come meet Noah."

Simone seemed to notice the two other men with them, men I didn't recognize, when she let out a short growl. "No fair. That's cheating, you asshole."

Griff turned innocent eyes on her. "What? No, it isn't. Robbie and Jason wanted to tag along."

His husband rolled his eyes, and the two friends smirked while simultaneously seeming to each give me an assessing once-over. Why did I feel like fresh meat?

It soon became clear that Robbie and Jason were there to meet me. I wasn't quite sure how I felt about that. Put on the spot a bit, but also flattered in a way. I'd already promised myself to be open to meeting new people, and I decided to approach everyone as a potential friend at the very least. Robbie was adorable and bubbly while Jason seemed more reserved. The two of them were good friends, and I found out over the course of the evening, they were best friends with Sam as well.

Dante spoke up. "So, guys, what are we playing tonight?"

The room erupted as everyone tried to argue for their favorite game. I sat back and watched the interplay between spouses, siblings, and friends. Finally, the argument came to a standstill when a familiar trio of little old ladies entered the room. I remembered them from the sex toy party. They'd made me laugh so hard, I almost busted a bottle of Tube Lube all over the place.

The tiniest of the old ladies squawked when she saw me. "Lordy, it's the massager man."

Another one cried, "OPAH!"

The tallest of the three, Irene I believed, smiled sweetly at me. "Just the man we wanted to see. You wouldn't happen to have a spare Satan's Ladyfinger would you? I think we want it in piccolo size."

I blinked at her before my mouth was able to respond. "Ah... ah... no, ma'am. Sure don't. I didn't bring any of my..." I coughed. "Products with me tonight."

"Dammit," Teddy muttered.

I felt my face ignite and tried my hardest to change the subject. No dice.

"Oh wait," Jason said with a big grin. "This is your gadget guy?"

Sam nodded. "The one and only. Noah the Naughty Toy Tinkerer."

"No," I squeaked. "Just Noah. Noah Campbell."

The third old lady narrowed her eyes at me. "Nothing wrong with claiming your love junk, little boy. Own it."

I glanced around at the faces of the Marians in a desperate hope of being rescued by someone. Anyone would do. Finally, my eyes landed on a new face. An attractive man with a bit of a baby face. He looked really sweet. Sweet and *safe*.

Jamie stood up and welcomed him. "Josh! Over here. There's someone you need to meet."

I felt my breathing speed up as I wondered if Jamie had invited this guy here to meet me. Were they all fucking crazy?

"Goddammit," Simone blurted. "No. No fucking way. Not fair. All of you suck."

I turned to Jude, who was still sitting calmly next to me. "What's happening?"

He shook his head in a pitiful gesture of disappointment. "My family doesn't know when to let well enough alone. Sorry, Noah."

"I don't... I..." I stammered.

The sound of the doorbell rang into the cacophony, and Mrs. Marian came bustling into the room from the direction of the kitchen. "Oh good, that must be Hayworth. I promised Mav I'd introduce him to Noah."

"Jesusfuckingchrist," AJ said on a sigh. "What about Jordan? We should have invited him to game night too."

I didn't remember much after that. It was a whirlwind of being polite and smiling— trying my hardest not to lose my cool and reminding myself it wasn't my job to balance attention on each eligible bachelor in the room. By the time I walked out the front door a few hours later, my head spun and I had a calendar full of "fun holiday activities" planned with several people.

Rain poured down when the Uber driver dropped me off in front of the apartment building. I tried to dash into the building without getting soaked, but a truck passed by and shot ice-cold rain water all over me. Perfect.

I threw the apartment door open with a dramatic groan and a squish of wet shoes. Luke was working on his laptop at the kitchen island. His eyes widened at the sight of me, and he jumped up to make a fuss. I must have looked like a mutt who'd been shoved the wrong way through a car wash.

"Take off your clothes," he said.

I jumped back, staring at him like he'd lost his fucking mind. After the aggressive innuendo and setup nature of my evening, everything had begun to sound sexual. "What?" I croaked.

He blinked. "You're soaking wet, Noah. I thought you might want to remove your dripping outerwear. You know, jacket, sweater..." The man's eyebrows were raised in question. "You okay?"

I blew out a breath. "Yeah, sorry. I just... I just had a strange night, that's all."

Luke reached for my jacket and began gently peeling it back from my wet sweater. "God, you're freezing and drenched. What the hell happened? I didn't even know it was raining."

"I can't feel my hands," I said with a chuckle. "And I'm Canadian."

"Being Canadian doesn't make you a superhero," he muttered as he hung my coat on a doorknob. He returned to help me pull off my sweater. "Kick off those shoes, and let's get your socks off."

I did as he asked—not really paying attention to what was happening because I was busy replaying the crazy night in my head. The Marian family had been absolutely bonkers crazy. But in the very best way, and I was beginning to think their desire to set me up was an honest attempt to help me meet people in my new town.

I realized Luke was mumbling something while he helped me dry off.

"Reminds me of the time you fell off the dock at the marina and scared the shit out of everyone," he said. "Your lips were so blue I thought your mom was going to have a heart attack when she got there."

"Oh my god. Yeah. I think I was more scared than anyone else. Mike Nelson pushed me in on a dare. As if a twelve-year-old pushing an eight-year-old over was something to brag about," I muttered.

"He was an asshole. The guy used to try flirting with Rosalie even when she and Scott had been dating for months."

That sparked a memory and I laughed. "You're right. Then Rose would use Mike to make Scott jealous. One year Scott didn't ask her to the school dance, so she convinced Mike to ask her instead. Scott got so mad he broke Mom's glass mixing bowl. It was Christmas, and

I thought she was going to rip his head off. Instead, she didn't let him have any of the gingerbread cookies she made."

Luke smiled. "I remember. She still let me have them though."

I was rendered a little stupid by the feel of his hands as they rubbed mine dry between them. "No, she didn't."

He turned away to get a couple of dry kitchen towels from a drawer but looked over his shoulder to respond. "What do you mean? I remember eating them and taunting Scott with them."

"I gave you mine," I admitted, distracted by the sight of his firm butt filling out his trackpants as he leaned over to reach the towels in the back of the drawer.

The silence sparked around us as he stepped in close and started to rub my hair dry with one of the small towels.

"You did?" he murmured. One corner of his lips turned up in a small smile. "Thanks. I never knew."

"Feels good," I breathed. "I should be thanking *you*."

"Mm," he said absently. "You need a keeper."

"Huh?"

"Someone to watch over you and keep you from getting mauled and soaked and... you know. Other things," he explained while slowing his ministrations and brushing droplets off my cheeks with his large, warm palms. His touch was like a shot of the smokiest bourbon—smooth and intoxicating. I stood there drinking it in and letting the warm bubbles of his attentions relax me. I leaned into him a little farther, seeking his warmth. His cheek barely grazed mine as he leaned in to reach the back of my damp neck with the towel.

I felt his hot exhales against my ear and noticed my own breathing stop.

"Luke?" Did I whisper it? Did I even utter the name out loud?

How wrong I'd been. It wasn't his touch that was warm and intoxicating. It was his voice.

"Noah," he said slowly in a deep rumble that rocketed straight through my heart to my dick. "Let's get you out of these clothes."

6

LUKE

What the hell was I supposed to do when I had Noah exhausted and cold in my arms? Everything inside me was begging to take him to my bed, strip him down, and curl around him until he warmed back up.

But this was Noah, for god's sake. *Little Noah.*

The minute I felt my dick respond to the mental image of a naked Noah Campbell in my bed and in my arms, I saw the image of a pissed off Scott Campbell storming into the room and shooting me in the fucking face with a military-grade firearm.

So I did the right thing and led him to his room. I waited patiently outside his closed door while he changed into warm sweats before I led him back to the kitchen for a cup of hot tea.

"You want to talk about the family night you went to at that guy's parents' house?" I asked when we sat on opposite ends of the sofa. I grabbed a corner of the fuzzy blanket folded nearby and shook it out to throw over his legs.

"Thanks," he said with a smile. "No, I don't want to talk about it. Just know that they tried to set me up on like a million blind dates at the same time. It was exhausting."

"You're kidding? Why exhausting?"

He finished a sip of his hot drink and set the mug down on a stack of magazines on the end table. "I didn't want anyone's feelings to be hurt, so I tried to pay equal attention to each of the guys they'd invited over without giving anyone the idea I was interested. I felt like the guy on a gay bachelor show, except there weren't any roses to give out. Only phone numbers."

"God. That does sound exhausting. So... no one interesting?" Yes, I was fishing. So sue me.

He shook his head. "No, that's not what I meant. They all seemed like great guys actually."

My stomach dropped while he continued.

"I just didn't want to play favorites."

I paused for a beat to avoid sounding like a psychopath. "You going to go out with any of them?"

Noah nodded. "Yeah. I made plans with each of them before I left, I think," he said absently.

"What? *What*? Each of them? How many dates did you—" I realized my voice was louder than I'd intended when I saw his eyes bug out at me. I cleared my throat. "Sorry. I meant... really? That sounds interesting."

He looked at me in confusion. "You don't think I should have accepted them? But, I just thought..." He pulled his mug back to the front of his chest like a protective shield. "I just thought if I only accepted a date with the one guy I liked best, it would hurt the other guys' feelings. And I could use some friends." He sounded insecure now, and I hated it.

I felt like a complete ass.

"That's very thoughtful of you, Noah. I didn't realize you were afraid of hurting their feelings."

We sat in silence for a few moments sipping our drinks before my mind replayed something he'd said.

"There was one guy you liked best?" I asked.

His face broke into a smile. Oh hell. I braced myself.

"Yeah. I mean, he seemed nice. And he was cute as heck."

"And you're going to go on a date with him?" I picked at a funky thread hanging off the end of my lounge pants' drawstring.

"He's a park ranger at Alcatraz. He said he wants to take me somewhere that's as beautiful as me. Is that cheesy? That's cheesy." Noah's face bloomed red and his neck got blotchy.

Yes, that's fucking cheesy as hell. What a player.

"No, that's sweet, Noah," I said. I wanted him to feel appreciated. He *was* beautiful. Even if the other man was just saying it to get into Noah's pants, it didn't keep it from being true.

"Yeah," he said with a small smile on his face. "He seemed nice."

Nice. Well... I had to admit nice sounded...

Nice.

I blew out a breath.

Maybe nice is what Noah needed. He certainly *wanted* nice.

Who the fuck wanted nice? I wanted fire and heat. Grab and clench. I wanted the roller-coaster ride that yanked all attention away from real life and threw you one hundred percent into the high and the thrill. Left you gasping and bug-eyed at the *oh shit* of it all and wondering when, for the love of god, you could get on and ride it again.

I wanted Noah.

I heard him say something else but couldn't make it out.

"Hm?"

"I think it'd be good to date somebody *nice* after Gord. I deserve it, Luke."

I glanced up at the defensive tone of his voice. "Of course you do."

"I do," he said a little quieter.

"What happened with Gordon, Noah? Scott just said you two broke up. He didn't explain why."

He flapped his hand at me. "I overheard him talking smack about me to his friends. It's embarrassing. I didn't tell Scott."

"Tell me," I said gently.

He huffed out a breath through his nose and looked away, fingers twisting the soft fabric of the blanket in his lap. The warm flickers from the gas fireplace danced light and dark across his features.

Noah really was something to look at—lovely like a familiar but treasured keepsake. Having him there with me was like being in the presence of a little bit of home and a whole lot of temptation.

"Gord's a fighter pilot. You know how they are," he said with a shrug. "Big ego."

"And?"

He looked off toward the large windows that overlooked the city. When he spoke, his voice sounded smaller. "He told his friends they should all consider dating a nurse too so they could be taken care of at home. I thought it was sweet at first, you know? But then he called me the 'little woman' and started describing in graphic detail how I 'took care' of him at home. *Sexually.* And he told them how he'd conned me into ironing his clothes and doing the cooking and cleaning in our apartment. As if I did those things because I was some idiot or a 1950s housewife rather than because I cared about him. God. I thought my heart was going to crack wide open when I heard him bragging about those things. And I was humiliated in front of those other men on top of it. How the hell was I supposed to face them again?"

As he spoke, my stomach began to twist, and I wanted to fucking kill Gordon Ewing.

"Oh god, Noah. I had no idea. You said Scott doesn't know?"

His eyes widened. "Hell no. He'd kill the bastard. Jesus, no."

Noah was right. If anyone so much as harmed a hair on that kid's head, Scott would pulverize them. But Gordon was his brother-in-law —Rose's brother.

"Then what does he think happened between you two?" I asked.

He sighed. "I told him a different truth. That I needed to get out of Cold Lake for my sanity. He knows I never planned on staying, and obviously Gord can't leave his post."

"What did you tell Gordon? How did he take the breakup?"

Noah shook his head and looked down at his hands again. "I never told him. I just left."

I stared at him. "Are you kidding?" Served the bastard right. Part of me wanted to laugh my fool head off, but the other part didn't want to laugh when Noah was so clearly upset about it.

"Not kidding. I left him a note," he said defensively. "It's not like I just vanished into thin air."

"What did your note say?"

Even though his face was angled down at his lap, I could see a tiny grin appear.

"It had the name and phone numbers listed of a maid service, pizza delivery, dry cleaner, and a nurse I know who's always wanted him. Then I added a note at the bottom suggesting his needs would be covered just fine in my absence as long as he had that list."

I barked out a laugh. "You did not."

"Did too," he said with a grin. "Fuck him."

"Fuck him very much," I agreed, noticing the stubborn set of his jaw. "I'm in awe of you."

He rolled his eyes. "Yeah, well... I'm not sure it was smart."

"Why not?"

"Because I took the absolute first job I could find, and it's shit."

"Well, that at least explains why you took a job selling kitchen gadgets when you're a registered nurse. I didn't want to pry, but I did wonder," I admitted.

"I have a job offer from St. Vincent's Hospital, but I have to pass the NCLEX first to get my US license. It's a process that takes ten to twelve weeks. They think I can start at least training at the hospital around the first of February. I have some savings, but I didn't want to just turn up without a job for the next couple of months. So that's why I took the temporary sales job."

"Ah, that makes sense. Sounds like a good plan, but you know I don't mind you living here rent free as long as you need, right? Don't feel like you need to do the gadget sales because you feel like I—"

"I don't," he said quickly. "But thanks for saying so anyway. I wouldn't be able to look at myself in the mirror if I didn't have some kind of work to do in the next few months, though. This is fine."

We sat in silence for a while finishing our drinks. When I stood up to take the mugs to the sink, I noticed Noah had fallen asleep curled up under the blanket on the end of the sofa. I deposited both of our mugs in the kitchen and then returned to help him move to his bed.

"Let's get you to bed," I murmured, leaning over him to pull the blanket off. He didn't stir, so I put my hand on his shoulder to give it a gentle shake. "Noah, baby."

I froze. My throat tightened around the stupid endearment as I stared at his sleeping face, hoping like hell he hadn't heard me. What the fuck had I been thinking?

Of course I knew exactly what I'd been thinking. That he was mine. I wanted him. But not in the way of wanting to simply fuck his brains out and leave him. Not that I didn't want to fuck his brains out, because I did. I definitely did want that. But I wanted to take care of him too. Dry him off and welcome him home. Fix him a cup of tea and rub his feet after a long day. Listen to him talk about the funny people he met at work. Share a meal with him and watch old movies together.

Never in my life had I felt that way. I wondered if it was some kind of complex manifestation of the obligation I felt toward my best friend to take care of his little brother. Was that somehow making me feel maternal toward Noah?

He stirred in his spot on the sofa.

"Luke?" he asked in a groggy voice. "I think I fell asleep. Sorry."

I reached out a hand to help him up. "Come on. I'll help get you to your room."

THE FOLLOWING AFTERNOON, I was alone in the apartment working on my laptop when I heard a commotion on the other side of my door. It was Noah, and he was absolutely three-sheets-to-the-wind plastered.

And I thought I'd never seen anything more adorable in my entire fucking life.

Until I realized he was surrounded by mountains of colorful cocks.

7

NOAH

On Sunday afternoon I was scheduled to run my first Love Junk party without Sally's help. I'd already shadowed her at four events throughout the week, so I'd become familiar enough with the products and presentation to know I'd probably be fine. The problem wasn't the Love Junk. It was the venue.

Somehow Sally had convinced Sam Marian to contact one of his old friends at a gay club called Harold and Richard's and arrange for the go-go boys there to host a Love Junk party with me as their consultant. I'd known I was running a party this weekend, but I hadn't found out until Friday's game night that it was for some half-naked hotties at a club.

I was thankful the party was during the afternoon hours so I at least wouldn't be competing with the loud music and half-drunk clientele.

Once I got there, I discovered fairly quickly I'd been wrong about the half-drunk clientele.

"Ssssup, handsome?" a boy in a leather harness and hot pink booty shorts slurred in my direction. "Come on over here and let us get a good look at you."

Ignoring the temptation, I glanced around to find the person in charge. I'd been told to report to a man named Julio. After spotting a man holding a clipboard behind one of the bars, I decided to take a chance.

"I'm looking for Julio?"

The man's friendly face opened up in a smile. "You found me. Noah, right?"

"Yes," I said with relief. "That's me. Where would you like me to set up?"

He set down the clipboard. "Follow me. We have a special events room. Thank you so much for agreeing to do this on short notice. We came up with an idea for a toy night during the holidays, and Sam said he knew just the guy to help get us started with some stuff."

I wheeled my large suitcase of samples and demo products through the dim hallway to a set of double doors. The club looked odd with its overhead lights on and I was reminded of how much the magic of a club atmosphere came from the people rather than the club itself.

"What kind of toy night?" I asked.

Julio gestured to a couple of long L-shaped sofas with a huge low coffee table set up between them. I rolled my bag to a stop and unzipped it to pull out my stuff.

"We were thinking it would be a sexy version of Oprah's Favorite Things. You know, engage the crowd by giving a bunch of stuff away and demoing some products on stage. The idea is to get the guys excited about gifts for themselves or their partners. All of the proceeds on our end will go to a local gay youth shelter. Sally said if we do it, you can handle the actual orders that night." He laughed. "I'm not sure she has any interest in being here during a long-ass Saturday night and accepting orders paid for in sweaty singles."

I felt my face redden on her behalf. "Fuck no," I blurted. "I think she'd rather die."

Julio took a moment to assess me. "And what about you?"

"What about me?" I asked.

"Would you rather die?"

I was taken aback. What did he mean by that? "Excuse me?"

His smile was disarming. "You seem a little nervous. Can I get you a drink?"

I blew out a breath. "Yeah. Maybe that would help. Sorry, I'm new at this."

He grinned again and clapped me on the shoulder. "No worries, friend. We'll have a great time. The guys are going to love you."

I gulped as hot men of all shapes and sizes began to trickle into the room and many sets of eyes roamed over me like I was one of the Love Junk products. There was just enough clothing between all of them to dress one medium-sized human.

"That's what I'm afraid of," I muttered under my breath.

By the time I stumbled out of there a few hours later, I'd made as much in one afternoon as I'd made in a week as a nurse back home. I was riding high with the adrenaline of sales success, the positive attention of a room full of gorgeous men, and the knowledge that I could handle a Love Junk party on my own without Sally. I'd also booked three additional parties through the people in attendance as well as finalized details for the enormous Harry Dick's Toystravaganza event (which they really wanted to call "Come Stuff Our Jocks night" but I refused to play along). The only problem was that I'd gotten just a teeny bit drunk in the process.

Julio hadn't brought me a beer like I'd assumed. He'd brought me shots. And then every time someone bought something (or said the word dildo, or made a blow job gesture, or pretty much breathed in or out), they offered me more shots.

Thankfully, Julio had put me in a taxi back to my apartment. Well, back to Lukie's apartment. Lukie's... Lu*ke's*, *Luke's* apartment. Not my apartment. No. Not mine. Luuuuke's.

Lukie Baby's. Loooookes.

I sighed and hiccuped the whole drive home. For some reason when I got up to the apartment, the door wouldn't open. I tried the knob lots of times. And, like, every which way I could think of.

Jiggling it, shaking it... poking at it a little. I even tried sliding it sideways the same way you unlock an iPhone, but that didn't work either. I kicked it with my toe in frustration.

Stupid fucking broken door.

Finally, I realized I'd just have to wait there. Wait until someone noticed my dilemma or until I sobered up—one of the two. For some reason, it didn't occur to me to call or text Luke.

Luke.

I sighed again.

Luke is so fucking hot. Sooo fucking hot. And smart. And successful.

I sighed some more.

I wish I could lick him.

What if I licked him? I wonder if he'd freak out. He'd probably majorly freak out. No one wanted to get sex-licked by someone they thought of as their baby brother.

What if it was just a tiny sex lick? Like a teeny, tiny, itty-bitty—

I fell backward into the apartment.

"Luuuuuke!" I cried in happy surprise. "You're here!"

He looked at me with a very odd expression on his face.

"I live here."

"Oh. Right. No, I know. But I—"

He sniffed the air. "Are you *drunk*? I thought you were working."

"I was. I am. I mean, I drank. I was drinking. A working drink. I mean... wait. It was a drinking work. Like a working lunch. But with drinking. And, ah, no lunch really." I stopped and thought that through. "Huh. There wasn't any food at all. That was the problem. Those parties usually have food. Well, they usually have cocktail wieners at the very least. Why does everyone think that's the most original idea ever for their sex party? I dunno, but they do."

I noticed Luke's eyes widen in shock, and I thought I'd said something embarrassing and revealing. I played back my words. Nope, I didn't let on a single thing hinting I sold Love Junk instead of kitchen gadgets.

"A sex party? Jesus Christ, what the hell are those?" Luke asked as his eyes landed on something behind me.

I swiveled my gaze in the direction he pointed and saw piles and piles of dildos all over the hallway. There were dozens of Cock Collars, Sac Spinners, and individual sample packs of Cum Gum spread among them. It was a veritable cornucopia of sexual delights.

I looked back at Luke in a high-octane fog of embarrassment and intoxication.

"Would you believe me if I said they were kitchen gadgets?"

8

LUKE

.

I couldn't even speak. How could I? Where exactly would I begin?

This was little Noah Campbell—a kid who couldn't possibly even know what a dildo was. He was too young for this sex stuff, but somehow he'd gotten ahold of... what, like a million variations of cock? I couldn't wrap my head around it. Why would any one guy need *that* much cock?

Of course, I knew he was plenty old enough for sex and had obviously had plenty of sex with his long-term boyfriend at the very least, but I still thought of him as the little boy I'd known back home.

Liar.

So maybe I didn't think of him as that little boy all the time anymore. But still. I'd known him when he was... oh fuck it. Clearly he knew his way around a dildo or two. Or thirty-seven.

"Noah?" I asked. It was all I could come up with on short notice.

"No," he said defiantly. "No. This is not happening, and you are not seeing this. Close your eyes. It's a mirage."

"Why are you swimming in cock?"

He looked away and muttered, "I wish."

"Let's get you inside. You're shitfaced."

"That... is accurate," he admitted, letting me stand him up and move him inside to the sofa. Once he crumpled into the cushions, I covered him with a blanket and returned to the hallway to clean up the products. There was a giant rolling suitcase there, and I stuffed as much of it into the bag as possible.

I couldn't help but peruse the merchandise as I did so.

If other cleanup jobs were as much of a turn-on as that one was, teenaged boys the world over would keep their rooms neat as a pin.

I finally made my way back into the apartment with Noah's big bag of tricks before closing the door behind me. It was nearly impossible to ignore the rock-hard *real* cock in my jeans after that, but I did my best. I had tried not imagining Noah using those items as I'd placed each one back into the suitcase, but it had proven impossible.

What would he look like with the Love Plug inserted in his tight little hole? How much would he squirm if I used the Quivering Cocksucker to edge him over and over for hours on end? As images swam through my head of Noah being debauched in every way imaginable by the toys, I realized every product was made by a company called Love Junk.

Wait.

I knew Love Junk. It was a home party company that sold these things through direct sales consultants. The same way Noah sold kitchen...

Fuck.

Fuck.

No.

I didn't mean to storm over and yell at him, but that's what happened.

"Noah, what the fuck?"

He blinked slowly until his vision seemed to clear. "Huh?"

God, he was so fucking cute, I could hardly stand it.

"You're selling Love Junk?" I blurted. "Why? Since when? And... and why?"

He rubbed his eyes and struggled to sit up straighter. I could smell the alcohol on him and wondered what the hell he'd been doing. I thought he'd been putting on a product demonstration.

I didn't wait for him to answer before I launched more questions. "If you were working, why are you drunk?"

He yawned, and all I could see were his plump lips stretching wide open. "I told you. The drinking work. The sex party. But I am hungry. Worked up an appetite with all those demonstrations."

My cock involuntarily jerked, and I clenched my jaw against the impulse to grab the kid and demand a private demo right here, right now.

Noah began to get up by reaching out for the sofa's armrest. He miscalculated, missing the armrest by a good ten inches and sliding back down into a heap in the corner of the cushions.

I held out my hand in a gesture for him to stay put. "Don't move. I'll bring you something to eat."

He sighed and smiled a sweet little smile with his eyes closed. "You're so hot."

I looked back at him in surprise and noticed his eyes fly open in shock. The flush of embarrassment began creeping up his neck as he scrambled to suck the words back in.

"Not you, I mean... whatever you're cooking. It's so hot. It's probably going to be so hot. Depending on what it is. Like... tea! The tea you're... Oh, might you please make me some tea? Hot, uh, tea. And then you'll *pour so hot*. That's what I said. *Pour so hot*. The tea."

I bit my tongue and turned back toward the kitchen to keep from barking out a laugh.

"One hot tea coming right up," I managed to get out before closing my eyes and feeling the grin overtake my face.

It wasn't until I was walking back into the living room with tea and a bowl of homemade vegetable soup that I remembered what he'd said about a sex party.

I held my tongue long enough to hand his mug over and make sure he took a few bites of the soup. When I spoke, I tried to remain calm.

"Noah, did you participate in a sex party at a night club this afternoon with a room full of go-go boys?" I noticed a throbbing begin in the area of my back teeth.

His eyebrows furrowed. "Yes. I told you. Remember you saw my junk?" His face flamed dark pink again before he croaked. "I mean, my Love Junk?"

I set my own tea down and turned to face him. I put a hand on his leg over the blanket and locked eyes with him.

"Was this an actual sex party or a sex *toy* party?"

His crinkled brow suddenly lifted into his hairline. "Oh, no! Oh god no. A sex party? Like, with sex? An orgy party? With... no. No! Jesus, Luke. God."

I squeezed his leg. "Calm down. Just making sure. You keep saying sex party, and I just wanted to—"

Now it was his turn to get mad. "Are you fucking kidding me? You thought— what? I was at a nightclub with a buncha dancers, offering my ass up to any of those guys who... I can't believe you thought I'd spent the afternoon just... you know. Doing *that*."

Which was cuter? Angry Noah or flustered Noah? It was a toss-up, really. But the image of Noah literally offering his ass up was doing things to me.

"Okay, okay. I'm sorry. You have to understand how confused I was when I thought you left here a few hours ago to sell some preppy dudes a bunch of whisks, and it turns out you were selling go-go boys a bunch of whips."

Noah began giggling at that. "Wisps. I mean, whisks. Whips. Not whisks. Hmm, that's a tongue-twister."

He blinked before smirking up at me. "Speaking of... I have a Tongue Twister. It's brand new; just came out last week in time for the holidays. Wanna see?"

Before I even had a chance to answer, he was up off the couch, lunging for the suitcase by the door. He leaned over the bag for a moment while he rifled through the items in search of what he wanted.

When he stood up, he brandished a neon green item made out of translucent silicon and covered in textured bumps.

"I'm afraid to ask..." I began.

"The Tongue Twister!" He returned to the sofa with a giant smile on his face. "Let me show you." He opened his mouth to put the device in it.

"It looks like a mouthguard you use in sports," I suggested. "What does it do?"

"It wybrates wike wiss," he mumbled around the item. He reached for my hand and singled out my index finger, sliding it into his mouth as if it was an everyday normal event. I felt the bumps on the device but I also felt the warm, wet welcome of Noah Campbell's mouth.

My cock sprang fully to life, and I swallowed a groan.

His tongue sucked me in while his eyes met mine, bright and shining green like Irish fields.

And then he turned on the vibration action and began to perform oral sex on my digit.

"Noah!" I yelped, jumping back and pulling my finger with me.

He blinked up at me in surprise and pulled out the toy. "What? What's wrong?"

In his drunken state, he had absolutely no idea what he'd done to me.

"It's, ah... it's just late and I think—"

Noah glanced around to find the clock on the mantle. "It's six o'clock. Dinner time." His face registered surprise. "Shit! I have a date tonight. Shit, shit."

"What?"

"You heard me," he said, standing up. "I should take a shower so I don't smell like a dance club."

"A date? With whom? Now? After you've already been drinking?"

God, why did I sound like such a big brother? That wasn't my job. I wasn't his big brother; I was his friend. Would a friend be okay with him going on a blind date already three sheets to the wind?

"Robbie. Or Jason," he said, seemingly confused. "Hm. I can't remember. One of them is taking me to dinner."

"But I cooked you dinner," I said with a frown. Wait, he was going on another date?

I didn't even think or wait for a response. Just blurted out like an idiot, "I'm coming with you."

Noah barked out a laugh. "No, you're not."

"I am."

He stared at me. "Why?"

"Because you're drunk, and if you insist on going through with a date with a practical stranger, you need someone along to make sure you don't get into any trouble."

"Won't you be a bird wheel?" His face was dead serious.

"You mean a *third* wheel?"

"That's what I said."

"I'll bring a date," I told him. "Victor's in town."

Noah looked away, and I noticed his jaw clench. I didn't think he liked Victor for some reason.

"Fine," he huffed. "I'm going to take a shower. If you're not ready by the time he gets here, you're not coming."

I couldn't help but poke fun at the fact he couldn't remember which guy it was. "By the time who gets here?" I asked innocently.

"Fuck you, Lukie," he shot back before shuffling off to his room. "Seven o'clock. Be there or... whatever."

It turned out to be a date with a man named Robbie, who was about the sweetest, most considerate guy I'd ever met. Which, of course, meant I wanted to kill him with my bare hands.

When I opened the apartment door to greet him, Robbie's eyes widened in recognition.

"Luke?"

Goddammit. I knew that guy. I'd met him at Pete Marian's house.

"Hi, Robbie, I thought that was you. How are things going?"

I invited him into the apartment and explained that Noah was a close friend of mine who was staying with me until he found his own place. A small voice in the back of my head tried to remind me now that I knew the date was with Robbie, I could trust Noah to go without me. I knew Robbie would never take advantage of him.

But of course, I didn't say any of that.

"Hey, Robbie, would you mind if a friend and I joined you two tonight?" I asked instead.

His eyes widened and he looked unsure. "Uh... sure? I guess?"

Just then, Victor came breezing through the still-open doorway decked out in his finest high-end fashion as if he'd just stepped off the pages of *Vogue*. I was pretty sure Robbie swallowed his tongue and simultaneously popped a boner.

Victor's smile was like a crocodile's. "Well, hello there, cutie. Who do we have here?"

"Victor, this is Robbie. He's here to take Noah out. We're going to join them for dinner," I explained.

Victor's eyes roamed up and down Robbie's small body as if determining where he would start snacking on the guy.

"Yes, please," Victor murmured under his breath.

I tried not to roll my eyes. "I'm going to go check on Noah to see what's taking him so long."

When I got to Noah's door, it was open just a crack. "Noah? It's me. You almost ready? Robbie and Victor are here."

I heard sniffling and peeked in through the crack. Noah was sitting on the far side of the bed facing the wall. He was hunched over, crying into his hands, his phone abandoned on the bed next to him.

Without thinking, I pushed the door open and raced to his side. "Noah, what's wrong? Did something happen?" I sat down on the bed next to him and put my arm around his shoulders.

He blinked up at me, his wet lashes framing vibrant green eyes. "Mom and Dad had to put Murphy down."

Murphy was the Old English sheepdog his family had had since he was a puppy and Noah was only fourteen. Noah had been so lonely after Scott left the house, his parents had brought home a puppy to keep him company. Murphy was as much a Campbell as Noah and Scott were.

"Oh baby," I murmured, pulling him into a full hug. "I'm so sorry."

Once his face landed against my neck, he took one deep breath in and then broke down completely.

9

NOAH

After hearing the sad news about Murphy from my mom, the rest of the night was a blur. Between drinking too much at the club and then crying my eyes out over Murph, I was in no mood to go out on a date.

Luke took care of everything while I stayed in my room and changed into comfortable pajamas. I found out later that Victor had been pleased as punch to take Robbie out to dinner without Luke and me.

"Doesn't that upset you?" I asked Luke a little while later.

We were sprawled out on opposite ends of the sofa with a roaring fire and old holiday movies playing on the television. Luke had assembled a giant selection of junk food and spread it out all over the coffee table in front of us. He was on his third bourbon while I sipped on Bailey's Irish Cream over ice.

Needless to say I was in heaven.

"Why would it upset me?" Luke asked before throwing a handful of cheesy popcorn in his mouth. With each drink, I'd noticed him relax exponentially.

"Dude, your boyfriend took another guy out to dinner," I pointed out.

"He's not my boyfriend. I've told you that before."

"You've been sleeping together regularly for months," I said, trying not to crack my teeth or imagine them naked together in bed.

Luke turned to me with a curious glance. "Why are you snarling?"

"I'm not snarling," I snarled.

"Are too. It's cute."

"Fuck."

"Noah, he's just a friend with benefits, okay? I don't have time for relationships. The law firm is my ball and chain," he clarified. "Besides, if I was going to have a relationship, it wouldn't be with a guy who drools over every attractive man in the room. I'd prefer to be with someone who thought *I* was the attractive man in the room."

"You are," I said without thinking.

I looked away as my face heated.

"Thank you. But you're wrong. You're the attractive man in this room," Luke said in a low voice.

I looked back at him, wondering if I'd see the joke on his face. What I saw was definitely not a joke. It was intense and hot—a look filled with desire and promise.

My heart began to stutter as I focused on his lips. They were wide and full, deep rosy red surrounded by dark stubble that made me breathe heavy.

"Luke?" I asked in a breathless voice as I found myself moving toward him.

"Yes."

It wasn't much, but it was enough. I kept my eyes on him as I approached, climbing onto my knees before straddling his jean-clad hips where he sat on the sofa. I continued my momentum until our faces were inches apart. Luke's eyes were laser-focused on my mouth.

"I just need to..." I murmured as my lips inched closer to his.

His eyes were dark with blown pupils, and his face was flushed. Luke's hands came up to cup the sides of my face, and I marveled at how strong and warm they felt against my skin.

The man smelled like my favorite cologne mixed with soap and home.

"We shouldn't," he breathed against my mouth. "Noah, please."

I wasn't sure which he actually meant—*shouldn't* or *please*—but the latter was enough to make me arch into him and take what I wanted, throw every sane thought of *could I* and *should I* and *would I* right out the window.

When I moved the last fraction of an inch to close the distance between our mouths, I felt like the entire universe heaved out a sigh of relief.

Finally.

My lips were on Luke Holland's lips.

And they were fucking glorious.

They nibbled against mine, tongue gently teasing along the edges until I opened and let him in. And then it was everything all at once. The smoky bourbon taste of his tongue. The strong grasp of his hands in my hair. The sound of bells tinkling from *It's a Wonderful Life* in the background.

Both of us were on fire, exploding with bursts of want and lust and *must take*.

I couldn't get enough of his hands on me and his mouth on mine. I pressed my body as close to his as I could and still whimpered into his mouth for more.

Luke's hands moved from my face to around my back and tightened into a possessive hold, one arm sliding down until I felt his large palm squeeze my ass. It felt so good I wondered if I might pass out.

"Mine," he rumbled into my mouth. "Mine, Noah. Understand?"

I wasn't sure he knew what he was saying in that moment, but I realized the answer to my earlier concern was *yes*. Yes, I was probably going to pass out.

I whimpered some more and felt my dick drool in my pajama pants.

"Yours," I breathed. "Please make me come, Luke."

"Fuck," he swore under his breath, grabbing me tighter around him and standing up. I held on with my legs wrapped around his waist and my arms around his neck. My lips continued to trail kisses along the edge of his jaw to his ear. The stubble on his cheeks raked across my tender mouth, but I didn't care.

As he walked, I felt the hard length of his dick shift against my ass through our clothes and I wanted them all off. Off now or as soon as humanly possible.

He strode quickly through the spacious apartment until he set me down on the foot of a massive bed. Luke's bed.

Luke Holland's *sex* bed.

I gulped. I'd only ever been in his bed a few times, and each of those were only in my dreams. Something about his innermost, private space caused me to pause. I wondered if he truly wanted me in there. If I was important enough or good enough to be there with him. If, in the sane light of day and without alcohol, he would actually be doing this with me.

"Your gorgeous green eyes make me feel stupid," Luke whispered. I looked up into his dark blue ones and saw the same intensity there seemed to be in them lately.

"I'm... sorry?"

"I can't think when I look at you, Noah. Can't fucking string two thoughts together," he said before peeling off my top. "Can't keep my eyes off you. Want you even though I shouldn't."

"Oh." All I could feel were his fingertips along my bare chest, my shoulders, my abdomen. "Oh god," I breathed.

Half my cock peeked out above the loose drawstring waistband of my pajama pants, and I was desperate for Luke to put his hands on it.

I wondered why I was being such a passive participant in this encounter. That wasn't like me at all. Was I intimidated by him? Afraid of doing something to upset him? Worried one false move would make him change his mind?

My hands came up to reach for his belt, and I began to unbuckle. From the sounds he was making, I knew I'd chosen the right place to start. He was barefooted and wearing blue jeans with a button-down shirt I'd already rucked up out of his waistband. Once I had his belt open, I worked on his fly until I was able to pull it open, revealing a line of dark hair down his belly.

I leaned forward to taste. My tongue ran along the trail slowly, causing Luke to hiss.

"Noah, you have no idea what you're doing to me," he warned low in his chest. His stomach muscles pinched and bunched as I drew the tip of my tongue along their defined edges. As I got closer to the top of his boxer briefs and stuck the tips of my fingers underneath to pull them down, I looked up at him through my eyelashes.

Just as I was getting ready to see the good stuff, a blaring ring shrilled from his pocket, scaring me half to death and causing Luke to curse and jump backward.

He seemed to shake his head to clear it before fishing the phone out of his pocket and staring at the screen.

"Fuck," he groaned, forcing his fingers through his hair in frustration. "It's your brother."

"No," I begged him. "Please don't answer it." I could see the apologetic look on his face. Like he had to answer it. And then I realized what was happening. He was using that phone call as a get-out-of-jail-free card. He'd been caught up in the passion of a moment but had been saved by the bell just in time. The realization left me numb.

Luke's tone was defensive. "What if it's important? What if he's upset about Murphy?"

I felt my stomach turn over. Damn him for being a thoughtful asshole.

After blowing out a breath in defeat, I stood up and grabbed my T-shirt to leave the room. There was no point in staying any longer. Whatever chance I'd had with Luke Holland went out the window the minute I heard him answer Scott's call.

"Hey, man," he said into the phone, as if nothing had happened. As if it was all just hunky-dory normal and Luke hadn't been about to shove his cock inside Scott's baby brother's desperate ass.

My goddamned brother—the ultimate cockblocker.

I wanted to punch him in the fucking mouth.

Instead, I took my sorry ass back to my room by way of the kitchen for a large glass of ice water. I knew I'd be feeling hung over the following morning if I didn't hydrate, and I sure as hell didn't want to have to sneak out there later and risk a humiliating run-in with Luke.

As I lay back on my own bed and thought back over the night's events, I knew it had been a mistake on Luke's part. He'd felt sorry for me. Or he'd been under the influence. Or just plain hungry for sex with anyone.

He hadn't meant it. Hadn't actually wanted me, Noah Campbell...

Correction, *little* Noah Campbell. The baby brother he'd never had. The kid he saw in his mind's eye with scraped knees and a desperate, youthful eagerness to fit in with the big kids. Who the hell was I kidding? Luke had never actually wanted me in his bed. Had it just been the beginning of a pity fuck?

I'd crawled across the sofa into his lap, putting him in the awkward position of having to let me down easy. Which he'd have had a hard time doing since I was practically family. Jesus. I was a fucking idiot.

I let out a sigh, hoping like hell I was wrong.

Maybe I was wrong. Maybe he cared. He'd made me dinner, after all.

But when two hours passed and he didn't come looking for me, I knew I'd been right the first time.

THE FOLLOWING two days were awkward as hell. Luke acted like nothing had ever happened between us. Whenever I tried to make eye contact with him, he looked away or busied himself with bullshit.

At first, I felt guilty and embarrassed, but then I remembered I was a grown goddamned man and could handle one failed hookup attempt without letting on that it had shattered me.

Which, of course, it had.

It was after work on Tuesday when I finally confronted him about it. He came home unusually early and seemed surprised to find me sitting at the dining table working on my laptop.

"Oh," he said, pulling up short. "I thought you said you were busy with, ah, work stuff today."

"I was. I did two parties, and now I'm entering all of the orders online," I responded. Then the child in me reared its ugly head, causing me to add, "I wanted to get it finished before my date arrives."

His head snapped up and he made eye contact with me for the first time in almost forty-eight hours. "What date? Really? Who? What date? I mean, ah... that's nice. Have fun."

I pursed my lips to keep from grinning in satisfaction. Maybe he wasn't as unaffected as I'd thought. Before he had a chance to escape to his room, I responded.

"It's a Spanish soccer player named Javier. He's taking me to see a game."

Luke's eyes widened. "You don't like soccer."

"No, you're right about that. But I do like soccer *players*."

I was pretty sure I saw his nostrils flare. "How did you meet *Javier*?"

He said the man's name as though it was thick poison on his tongue.

In order to hide my grin, I turned back to my computer and pretended to type. "It's another setup. That crazy family who insists I meet the love of my life before the holidays are over. I'm beginning to think I'm part of a bet or something." I chuckled, thinking of the funny group of people who'd gone out of their way to make me feel included.

Luke froze before speaking. "Noah. Is it the Marians? Are they the family who keeps setting you up?"

I turned back to him in surprise. "Yes. Blue and Tristan set me up with Javier. Apparently he did a photo shoot at their vineyard. You know the Marians?"

"Goddammit," he muttered shaking his head. "I'm going to fucking kill Pete."

"Pete Marian?"

He nodded and squeezed the back of his neck. "Yeah. He's one of my good friends and we work together." For some reason, he looked reluctant to admit it.

"So, I take it, I'm in good hands, then?" I asked. And if my tone sounded snippy, so be it.

He just nodded and shrugged. "I guess." He turned to walk toward his room, but I stopped him again.

"Luke, we need to talk about what happened."

Was Luke Holland blushing?

"Why?" he asked. "Nothing happened."

I stood up and faced him with my arms crossed in front of my chest. "Is that right? Nothing happened? So... no one explored anyone's teeth with their tongue? No one felt anyone's hard-on through their clothes?" As my frustrations with him bubbled over, my tone got sharper and his eyes widened farther. "No one called me baby? No one took me to their bed, planning to fuck me? Is that right?"

Luke's face was crimson by the time I'd built up a good head of steam. "Noah," he said, holding up his hands as if to stop the assault. "Wait. We should talk about this."

That's when I lost it.

"That's what I was suggesting! That's all I wanted to do. Make this awkward bullshit go away. I hate this. I hate it that you won't look at me. I hate it when you ignore me or leave the room because you can't stand the sight of me. Damn it, Luke, can't we just go back to the way things were before?"

"I've never heard you angry before," he said quietly.

I blew out a frustrated breath. "Not true. You and Scott wouldn't take me to see *Fellowship of the Ring* with you at the theater. I threw a massive tantrum and tried to beat the shit out of both of you."

Luke leaned his head back to laugh. "You were such a brat. As if we were taking a preteen with us to the movies. We had dates, for god's sake."

I rolled my eyes. "Scott had Rose. That didn't count. And you took Milton Laurens. What a douche."

Luke studied me, his lips curling up on the sides as my words sank in. "You remember who I took on one date when you were twelve?"

I felt my skin betray my embarrassment at being caught out. "No," I said stupidly.

"You do. What, were you jealous?" he teased.

"No," I repeated.

Of course I was. I'd had a crush of some kind on Luke Holland since I was an embryo probably. At least it felt that way. It hadn't always been sexual, of course. I'd just wanted to be near him. Hang out with him. He was smart and clever and sweet and kind. Luke was just a good person. Always had been.

"Never mind," I muttered. It didn't matter anyway.

He stepped closer to me and began to reach out a hand to me before stopping and letting it drop back by his side. "It's not that I can't stand the sight of you, Noah," he said softly. "It's that I can't stand seeing something I want so badly but can't have."

My heart plummeted into my stomach and my lungs ceased to function.

What in the world did he mean by that?

"Why can't you have it?" I asked, my cracking voice betraying me.

He pressed his eyes closed and I knew, just *knew*, what he was going to say.

"Don't," I spat. "Don't you fucking dare say it out loud. Tell me you don't like me, tell me you're not attracted to me, tell me you're not interested in a relationship, but *jesusfuckingchrist*, do not mention my goddamned brother."

Luke's eyes cast down to the polished wood floor and his words were broken.

"I'm sorry, Noah."

Before he could say another word, I'd grabbed my coat and bolted.

My one and only goal was to find the hot soccer player and get him naked as soon as possible.

Luke Holland could fuck the fuck off.

10

LUKE

That night and the following day at work were excruciating. Noah hadn't come home from his date with *Javier*.

Hadn't called, texted or given a shit of any kind that I might have been worried about him. I'd finally swallowed my pride and picked up the phone to text Blue. After making four or five or seven attempts at wording it in such a way as to not sound like either a concerned parent or a possessive asshole, I finally gave up and put my phone down.

I had to accept the fact he'd stayed the night with the professional soccer player. Some random stranger had been the one to take him to bed. And it wasn't like I could complain. I'd had my chance and had blown it all to bits.

When I'd heard Scott's voice on the other end of the line, I'd felt a twist of guilt in my gut. There I'd been, getting ready to do filthy things to his baby brother. The guy he'd trusted me to look after and care for while he was in my city.

Instead, all I'd been able to think about was stripping him bare and pushing into his body. I could hardly look at Noah anymore without picturing what he would look like naked and writhing beneath me. I wanted him so badly my mouth began to fill with saliva now every time I looked at him.

It was awful. And I could never in a million years admit it to my best friend.

He'd been so worried about Noah's reaction to losing their family dog.

"How's he holding up?" he'd asked first when I'd answered his call.

At that point, the only thing "up" on Noah had been his rock hard cock, full and straining out of his pajamas with a fat drop of precum making its way down the side. Just remembering it made me hard.

I barely remembered the rest of the phone call. Scott worried about Noah. Me trying to reassure him Noah would be okay. It wasn't until Scott began asking for more information about Noah's job that I'd snapped out of my daze and shut the call down.

"Sorry, Scott, gotta go. My law partner's calling on the other line," I'd said in a rush before hanging up.

And now I was at work trying everything I could think of to concentrate on my job instead of worrying about Noah. My assistant, Jasmine, kept shooting daggers at me until she finally couldn't hold back anymore.

"Fuck it, what the hell's going on with you?" she blurted before she even came fully into my office. She closed the door behind her and crossed her arms in front of her. Her narrow gaze bore into me. "Spill it, sister," she demanded.

"Nothing. What? I'm just working on this brief for Samari."

She heaved out a dramatic sigh and dropped into my visitor chair. "Right. Luke, I've worked thousands of hours with you over the course of several years. You think I don't know when you're twisted up over something? What is it? I can help. You know I'm the master of solving problems."

I only debated internally before I realized she was right. She was the master of solving problems.

"Okay, there's this guy," I began. She immediately cut me off with an ear-splitting screech.

"I knew it! Tell me *everything*."

"Oh god, calm yourself, woman. It's not that big of a deal."

"I'll be the judge of that."

"You know Noah, my best friend's little brother who's staying with me right now?" I began.

"The one who's just finishing college?" she asked with a fake air of confusion.

"What? No. He's not some college kid. He's twenty-eight. He's a registered nurse who's been practicing for—" I noticed her *gotcha* face. "Fine, so he's not so little. What's your point?"

"My point is, you've never mentioned him without mentioning Scott or the fact Noah's the *little brother*. Have you ever thought about how that makes a grown man feel?"

"God, you sound like him now," I muttered.

Her grin was evil. "He sounds like a smart man. Continue."

"I really like him," I admitted in a rush.

She blinked at me and paused for a beat. "Duh."

"Can you be serious, please? What do I do about it? It's not right. We can't just... you know."

Jasmine tried hard to stifle a laugh but failed. "Why can't you? What's stopping you?"

I knew she'd kick my ass if I mentioned Scott again, so I just stared at her.

She shook her head. "Do you really think he wouldn't understand you falling for his brother? Do you think he wouldn't want both of you to be happy? Christ, I'd love it if my sister married my best friend. It'd make my life so much easier."

"I can't see Belle with Ricky," I teased. "She'd have to top and that would be a whole thing."

She couldn't help but laugh. "Can you imagine? One relationship could never handle so much high maintenance. It would explode. And her name isn't Belle. It's Kecia, as you well know."

"Jasmine, your other sisters are Ariel and Aurora. If Kecia isn't called Belle, it's only because your mom was on the good drugs when she was born."

"Kecia was first. Before Mom lost her fucking marbles and married a Disney freak," she grumbled.

"When you and Davi start a family, promise me you'll name your kids Moana and Kristoff."

She shot me the bird as she stood up, no doubt to answer a phone only she could hear ringing. "Stop tripping over your damned self and ask Noah out, Luke. Don't be an idiot."

"What happens when we break up?" I called after her.

"Don't break up," she called back with a smirk.

If only it were that easy. When had I ever not broken up with someone?

LATE THAT AFTERNOON I had a meeting with Pete. Once it was over and all of our other coworkers had left the conference room, I asked him the question I was pretty sure I already knew the answer to.

"Is my date for the party tomorrow night with Noah Campbell?"

I inwardly winced in anticipation for the confirmation.

Pete's eyes lit up. "Yeah, how'd you know?"

A long exhale escaped my lungs in a whoosh. "He's my roommate, Pete. You know, the guy who's staying with me? My best friend's—"

"No shit?" he interrupted with a wicked grin. "Wait. Didn't you say you were attracted to him?"

"No," I lied.

Pete wasn't buying it. "You did. So this is perfect. Fuck, I'm so going to be the favorite child at Christmas. But god, Ginger's going to be a complete ass with the I told you so's."

I shot him a look, and he laughed.

"C'mon, Luke. It's one law firm holiday party. If you don't want it to be a proper date, just introduce him around." Pete's eyes lit up with an idea. "I know! Introduce him to Gino or Trey."

I felt my teeth grind at the idea. "Are you crazy? Gino is a total slut, and Trey is the most boring person who ever lived."

He laughed. "He doesn't need to sleep with them, dude. He can just make some new friends. What about introducing him to Eden, that new paralegal? She just moved here from Louisiana. It might be nice for them to have another friend who's new in town."

"Stop trying to fix this," I warned. "He's met your loony toons family, so I'm pretty sure he's got plenty of people in his life right now."

"Good point. At least introduce him to Jasmine. She'll cut your balls off if you don't."

"You think I don't know that?" I muttered. "She's going to make best friends with him in the first thirty seconds and then use him to gang up against me. I can already see it all in my mind's eye."

Pete's wicked grin was punctuated with sparkling eyes. "This is going to be epic."

I stood and gathered my things from the conference room table. "It's not. It's going to be a disaster. It's going to hurt," I mumbled.

"Life is pain, highness," he quoted.

"Your girls are making you watch *Princess Bride* too often," I said with a laugh.

"I'm not complaining. That movie is epic."

I sighed and shot back, "You keep using that word. I do not think it means what you think it means."

Before I disappeared around the corner of the doorway, I heard him call out, "Hey, can your boyfriend get me a discount on a Slither Sheath or a Vlad the Impaler? Ginger made a list for Christmas."

I tried not to laugh as I turned my head to call out my response. "Sure, I'll ask him to throw in a sample bottle of Dick Drip as a bonus."

When I swiveled back around laughing, I came face to face with the head partner of our firm.

"Bertram," I coughed in surprise. I could see the older man's lips curve up in a smirk.

"Something you want to discuss, Mr. Holland?" he asked. "Might you need to see a doctor?"

I was never going to live that one down as long as I still worked for that firm.

Goddamned Pete Marian.

11

NOAH

I didn't sleep with Javier. The entire date had been a disaster, actually. I'd wrongly assumed he was taking me to a soccer game, when, in reality, it had been a hockey game. Which wasn't the problem at all.

I loved hockey. Loved it. I loved playing it, watching it, talking about it. I'd grown up surrounded by hockey in Cold Lake. Luke had been such a part of my family that we'd all been to many of the games he played, even when he'd been on the Cold Lake Ice juniors' team and traveled all over.

The problem was when a soccer star from Spain had tried to explain ice hockey to me as if I was a newbie to the sport. Not okay.

Javier was incredibly good-looking. When I'd met him at the restaurant for dinner before the game, I'd been pleasantly surprised to see how much hotter he was in person than in the photographs I'd seen online.

His accent had made him even sexier, and he'd been dressed in all high-end clothing. Being on a date with him made me feel a little bit like a celebrity, to be honest, and I'd begun the date in a great mood.

Until right about the first penalty call of the game.

The sexy Spaniard had leaned over and murmured into my ear,

"That means the guy will have to go into a penalty box and the team isn't allowed to replace him for a couple of minutes."

I'd nodded and smiled politely, assuming he hadn't intended his words to be as condescending as they were. I'd continued to suffer through his not-entirely-accurate explanations of cross-checking and high-sticking, still trying my best to maintain a pleasant demeanor until I couldn't hold back any longer. It hadn't been until the end of the first period when he tried to explain that it wasn't halftime, that I'd finally lost my cool.

"Javier, I know about hockey. I'm Canadian," I'd said for the third time. "I've played hockey and seen hundreds of games. One of my good friends was on the pro track before deciding to go to law school instead."

He'd blinked at me with chocolate brown eyes. "Oh, I didn't know."

"Well, I've mentioned it several times..."

"You also mentioned having seen soccer games, but you said you haven't seen a professional match."

"That's true," I'd said hesitantly, trying to make the connection.

"It's not the same."

"I've seen many Edmonton Oilers games. I know professional hockey," I'd told him. And then, of course, I'd felt guilty for being rude. "But I'd love to see a professional soccer game some time."

"The Earthquakes start the next season in March. I can get you tickets to see me play," he'd said with a hopeful expression.

"I'd love that, Javier. Thank you," I'd said sincerely.

We'd spent the rest of the game side by side outwardly cheering for the Sharks even though I'd been inwardly cheering for the Canucks. Once the game was over, Javier had driven us back to the city and asked if I'd wanted to go out dancing.

I'd thought about going home at a decent hour when the likelihood of Luke still being up was high. The idea of making awkward conversation in the apartment had decided it for me.

"I'd love to. Can we go to a club called Harry Dick's though? I know some guys there."

We'd danced a long time—enjoying the ability to let loose the stress from the game and just move to the thrum of the club music. I'd felt a kind of euphoria, and I'd realized it was the feeling of finally being where I was meant to be. I finally lived in San Francisco and was single and able to do anything or any*one* I wanted.

As Javier's hard, fit body had pressed and moved against mine on the dance floor, I'd imagined letting him take me into the bathroom for a blow job. I'd wondered what it would be like if I let him take me home and fuck me in a strange bed.

None of it had felt even remotely enticing. What I'd really wanted was to go home. To Luke.

Fuck Luke Holland. Really and truly. Fuck him.

When it had come time for the proposition, I'd politely declined Javier's offer, and instead, approached Julio behind the bar to ask if there was a hotel nearby.

He'd looked at me with kind eyes and offered for me to stay at his place for the night. While he wasn't any less of a stranger than Javier himself, I knew that Julio was good friends with Sam and Griff Marian, and my gut had told me it was okay to accept his offer of a place to crash.

I just hadn't wanted to face Luke again so soon. And lord only knew if it was due to embarrassment, anger, or just plain exhaustion.

Either way, I'd fallen onto Julio's living room futon like a sack of sleeping dogs and stayed there until almost noon the following day.

BY THE TIME Luke returned home from work on Wednesday evening, I had cooled off and resigned myself to returning to being just friends again. Honestly, as pathetic as it sounded... I missed him.

I missed his handsome fucking face and his sweet goddamned personality. I missed the stubbled dimples and the way he always asked me if I remembered to grab a warm hat before leaving the apartment.

It was his fault for being so... ugh. Whatever. I could do it. I could just be friends with him. I'd forget the implication he wanted me, and I'd pretend he didn't have that weird hang-up about me being Scott's brother. I'd just... deal.

"Hey," I said as he walked in and took off his coat. I was sitting in the kitchen working on my laptop.

He jumped and turned around to gawp at me. "You're... back."

"You're... observant," I teased.

He blew out a breath. "Thank god. I... I was worried. You didn't come home and I—"

"I'm fine," I said quickly, before he could sound any more caring and make me cry like an asshole.

He made his way toward the kitchen to get a drink.

"So," he began awkwardly. "How was the soccer game?"

I snorted. "Try hockey game."

He pulled out two bottles of beer, lifting an eyebrow as if to ask if I wanted one. I nodded.

"The Sharks? They played the Canucks, right?"

"Yes. And because I hadn't known the soccer season was already over, the guy assumed I knew nothing about sports. Spent the entire time trying to explain to me what a power play was."

Luke's deep laugh rang out loud in the smaller space. "No. Tell me that's not true."

"Can't."

"Noah, shit. I'd have given good money to see your face. What did you tell the guy?"

I took a sip of the cold beer and enjoyed the sharp taste of it going down. "I was polite at first. Then I finally lost my cool a little. It was fine after that."

"Must have been if you spent the night with the guy," Luke said. I noticed his eyes were focused on his beer bottle. The part of me that was still annoyed with him couldn't help but rear its bitchy head.

"We went dancing after that so there was no more talking. That made it easier."

I noticed his jaw tighten but otherwise there was no reaction.

Until he spoke with fake nonchalance.

"Oh... I see. Sure."

Clearly he was bothered by the idea of me hooking up with someone else. And if that was the case, *what the fuck?*

But it wasn't in me to lie to him.

"I politely declined his offer of a slumber party," I admitted softly.

His eyes flashed up to me—familiar blue pupils set below dark, confused eyebrows. Was that relief I saw?

"Yeah?"

"Yeah. I know a guy who works at that club, and I wound up crashing on his futon."

He sighed and put his hand on my shoulder. I tried valiantly to ignore the tingles I felt every time Luke touched me.

"I'm sorry you felt like you couldn't come home. That was shitty. I didn't handle myself well, and I'm really sorry," he said. After taking another sip of his beer, he turned to face me from the stool next to mine. "Actually, I'd like to ask you out on a date. Officially."

Either I tilted my head to study him or the entire fucking universe had just tilted on its axis.

"I'm sorry, what?"

Luke smiled, revealing the dimple I'd known all my life. "I know it's kind of an about-face, but I was wrong. Or confused... or just..." He shrugged. "Nervous, maybe? Anyway, I'd like to make it up to you. Tomorrow night."

I tried to remember what day it was. What year it was. What alternate universe I was in where Luke Holland was asking me out on an actual date.

"I'm sorry, what?" I asked again, squinting this time in hopes I could focus better when he answered.

The hand that had been resting on my shoulder moved up into the back of my hair, which meant there would be no focus happening whatsoever.

"A date, Noah. Tomorrow night. Dinner first, then there's this work thing—"

Reality came crashing in and I began babbling. "Shit! Fuck. No, I can't. I mean I can, but not tomorrow night. Well, let me see... maybe

I could. But then I'd have to let someone down, and I really don't want to do that. You see, I accepted another date for tomorrow night, and it's for someone's office party at work, and I'd hate to make the poor guy go dateless just because I'd much rather do you, I mean, do your date, I mean *be* your date." I stopped to take a breath and noticed he was holding back a laugh. "Shut up," I muttered. "You make my tongue wobble."

It figured that the hottest, nicest guy in existence would ask me out the same night I had other plans.

"Rain check?" I asked. My voice sounded high-pitched and desperate in my ears so of course, my skin began to heat up in a humiliating flush.

"No rain check. You're going out with me tomorrow night, Noah."

Bossy Luke. I kind of liked it.

"Oh. Well... hmm," I considered. It was most likely physically impossible for me to say the word *no* to Luke Holland, so I needed a moment to figure out how to let my blind date down easy.

His large hand moved around to cup my jaw. "No, I meant that *I'm* the person the Marians have set you up with for tomorrow night. That is, unless there's another Love Junk salesman they're friends with?"

I'd forgotten he knew the truth about my job. A sudden flash of memory assaulted me— drunken Noah using the Tongue Twister on Luke's long finger. Dear god. What other products had I demonstrated so helpfully to him that night?

"Oh Jesus," I breathed, remembering piles and piles of plastic peen. "You've seen my Love Junk."

Luke's eyes widened, which honestly, was becoming par for the course. "Not all of it, but I'd really like to."

"You should come to one of the parties I do," I blurted.

"Oh, *oh*. You mean your... Love Junk. Right. Sure. Well, I did see quite a bit of it the other night, but if there's anything in particular you'd like to demonstrate..."

This wasn't happening. I was pretty sure my face was going to incinerate and fall to ash on the floor. I couldn't possibly expect him to clean up the kitchen tile after me a second time in only a week.

"I need to go. Away. Like, right now," I admitted. "Probably to my room for a little while to dunk my face under some cold water. Do you... do you have a fire extinguisher by any chance?"

Luke's other hand came up to land on my face until both of his hands cupped my hot cheeks. His grin was as wide as his face and his deep blue eyes sparkled. "Stop. Take a deep breath. You're going to go to your room to get comfortable. Change into pajamas and meet me back in the living room for the Hallmark holiday movies you've been dying to watch but don't want me to know about. I'm going to watch them with you and pretend I'm just doing you a favor and that I don't really care about a single mother who can't afford gifts for her children. We're going to order Chinese and devour it in front of the television, and then we're going to eat the candy bars I found hidden in the freezer."

"Those are mine," I said halfheartedly.

He grinned. "I know. And you're going to share them with me because I'm a nice guy."

I stood up and moved toward my room. "Okay, fine. But you're snuggling with me under the blanket because otherwise I might cry when the single mom's new boyfriend plays Santa and brings all the toys."

Luke seemed to consider it for a minute before nodding. "It's a deal. But nothing more than cuddling. I have to save my energy for my hot date tomorrow night."

What hot date? I wondered. And then I remembered. The law firm holiday party with *me*. Luke was taking me out on an actual date.

Holy mother of god.

12

LUKE

Spending several hours with Noah wrapped in my arms under a blanket in front of the fire was like being edged by a master.

It didn't take long until I lay behind him with one arm under his head and the other wrapped around his middle. My knees fit against the back of his like they'd been made to live there. He felt amazing and smelled even better—a cross between my sandalwood soap and the fresh laundry smell of his T-shirt. It took all of my self-control to keep from nuzzling my nose deep into his neck to inhale the scent of him and wallow in it.

If someone asked me what movies we watched, I would have looked at them with a completely blank face and no idea of how to answer. The only scenes playing in my vision were the ones in my mind's eye of me sliding down his soft flannel pajama bottoms and thrusting my hard cock into his perfect ass.

It was all I could think about, all I could picture. My hand lay over his stomach and I could feel the faint outlines of firm stomach muscles through the old, worn fabric of his T-shirt.

At one point he stretched and shifted, bumping his ass back into my groin. I sucked in a breath and thrust my hips back into him before I could stop myself. His responding hum was enough to spike more blood flow to my hard-on. As if it needed help filling out.

It didn't.

We both pretended the little exchange didn't happen and went on watching the movie. But this time I had even less willpower than before. My hand moved slowly down to the hem of his shirt to sneak under it. I just needed to feel that warm skin without the cotton barrier.

First, I noticed the sparse, rough hair of his happy trail and ran my fingers gently up and down it from his low waistband to his belly button. I felt the muscles of his stomach clench, and I knew he was well aware of my touch.

After running my hand lightly all over his stomach and up to his chest, I noticed his breathing increase and his heart thunder under the skin of his chest. My own body responded the same way—my cock rock hard against the cleft of his ass.

"Luke," he breathed, grabbing my hand and forcing it lower, down under the loose drawstring waist of his flannel bottoms and over the silky skin of his throbbing dick.

"*Hngh*," I grunted, which was about as eloquent as I could get under the circumstances.

I ran my hand up and down the smooth stiffness before clasping the shaft and gently squeezing and tugging. The groan that rumbled out of him was like a fan to the flame of my own desire, and I thrust my hips into him.

"Fuck, Noah. You're so damned sexy," I murmured behind his ear, causing him to shudder against me. "I can't keep my hands off you. Don't want to."

Noah thrust his cock through my grasp and groaned again before looking back over his shoulder and responding. "What are we doing, Luke? I don't want to go down this road again if you're going to—"

I leaned in and shut him up with a kiss. His lips were soft and plump. Willing. My tongue traced them before sneaking inside his mouth. I pulled my free hand out of his pants and wrapped it around his middle to turn him. Once he was facing me, the kiss wheeled out of control. His hands gripped the sides of my neck so hard, I wondered if there'd be marks the following day.

I didn't care.

My mouth devoured his, doing everything in its power to consume him. He whimpered and groaned and panted into my mouth as my tongue assaulted his. He tasted like surrender, and I wanted it with a hunger I'd never felt before.

"Noah," I said against his wet lips. "What do you want, baby?"

"Huh?" His eyes were glazed—huge pupils rimmed by the narrowest of green rings. "A-anything. E-everything. Jesus," he stammered.

I felt my mouth turn up with the permission, and I began moving my kisses down his neck into the collar of his shirt.

Noah's hard cock arched up into mine, and I felt the promise of it. I wanted to taste it— to suck him off and watch his face as he let go in pleasure.

I pulled back to kneel between his legs on the sofa and fumbled for the remote, muting the volume so I could concentrate on every little sound Noah gave to me.

Once I threw the remote down on the carpet, I raked Noah's shirt up and slipped it over his head before doing the same to my own. His eyes locked on mine the entire time and I felt riveted to his heated gaze.

My palms landed against the cut muscles of his pecs and I squeezed his golden skin. "You have an amazing body, Noah."

His lips, swollen from my earlier assault, curved up in a shy smile. "Thank you."

Something about his simple acceptance of the compliment made my stomach flutter. He didn't roll his eyes or argue with me. He didn't fish for more compliments or complain that he needed to work harder on his physique. He simply allowed me to appreciate him.

I felt myself relax even further into him, leaning down to continue my trail of kisses down his chest, past the pinkish-brown disks of his nipples and back to the happy trail I'd already worshipped with my fingertips.

"So fucking sexy," I murmured against it as I ran my tongue down the golden brown hair. Noah's cock was pressing hard and insistent on my chest as I let more of my weight fall on him.

I slipped my fingers inside the waistband of his pajama pants and lifted my head to make eye contact with him. He looked like he was in some kind of trance. I lifted my brows at him in question and he nodded.

My eyes stayed on his as I pulled the pants off his long, toned legs. He was fucking gorgeous as hell, and I wanted to devour every inch of him. I heard the slap of his cock hitting his belly, and I felt a tug in my balls just from the sound of it. After pulling off the flannel pants and dropping them on the floor, I began at his ankle.

My mouth toyed with his skin the entire way up his legs—licking, nipping, kissing. Out of the corner of my eye, I could see his stomach muscles rippling and his thighs trembling, and I could hear his erratic breathing. When I reached his inner thighs, I thought he was going to pass out.

The power I had over him was intoxicating, and I wondered briefly if he knew it went both ways. In that moment, whether he realized it or not, Noah owned me. I couldn't have walked away from his naked body if I'd been offered the moon. I had to have it —have him.

By the time I dropped a wet kiss on one of his hipbones, he was panting. His cock jumped with every move I made, leaving a thin trail of sticky precum in that magical happy trail I'd worshipped earlier.

"Not gonna last," Noah admitted with a croak.

"Don't need to," I assured him before ghosting my nose and lips across his bouncing cock.

"Luke, please," he begged. He tried thrusting up toward my face, but I held him down with my arm across his hips. His hands scrabbled for the edges of the sofa cushion as if he was trying to keep from grabbing my face and shoving it onto his cock.

Hearing Noah beg for my mouth on him made my dick harder than it had ever been. His voice was hoarse and broken with desire, and he wasn't afraid to let me hear it.

I rewarded him by running my tongue slowly up from his balls to his tip, circling my tongue around the bubble of precum in the center, and then taking his entire length down in one move.

"Fuck! Holy fuck—ohmygod. Oh Jesus. Luke," he cried. His hands finally found my hair and threaded into it quickly as if holding on for dear life.

I loved the feel of his fingers in my hair and his cock head in my throat. After humming my happiness, I pulled off and sucked and licked his balls. Noah's legs fell wider apart and I caught a glimpse of his hole beneath his sac.

After quickly sucking my thumb into my mouth, I ran the wet pad of it around his hole while I sucked his shaft back into my mouth.

That was all it took. With no time for warnings, and honestly, no need for them either, he shot long and hot into my throat. I did my best to watch him as I swallowed his release.

Noah's flushed face, bright but hooded eyes, and plump lips open in surprise were almost as beautiful as the sounds he made.

Fuck, he was gorgeous. Just watching him come had set me right on the edge. I fumbled my hand into my own pajama pants and ran the precum around my cock until I took a few quick pulls to join him in his release.

After reaching for my discarded T-shirt to wipe my hand off, I began making my way back up his body with more kisses, slowly enough to give him a chance to catch his breath. I tried to ignore the residual wet spot in my pants and concentrate on the man blissed out beneath me.

After a moment, he seemed to become more aware and grabbed me under the arms to pull me up faster.

"C'mere," Noah murmured, pulling my face in for a kiss when I was lying fully on top of him again. We kissed slowly, almost lazily, before ending up with our foreheads pressed together and eyes locked again.

What was it about him that made me comfortable just staring at him?

"Thank you," I said softly, not wanting to break the spell.

"For what? You're the one who did all the work," he admitted with a chuckle.

"For letting me touch you like that, for letting me see you come."

His face flushed deeper pink, and his eyes flitted away. "You're welcome."

My heart hammered in my chest. Despite him feeling put on the spot or nervous or whatever it was he was feeling, he allowed me to thank him. Again.

I stared at him some more before he spoke up.

"What?" Noah asked with a grin. "You look like a psycho."

"I'm just trying to visually measure you for a shallow grave, no big deal." I grinned back as he brought his hand down on my pajama-clad ass.

"It's winter. No grave digging, remember?" he teased.

"We're not in Cold Lake anymore. You can dig in California in winter," I corrected.

Now he had both hands on my ass and was testing out the fit of my cheeks in his hands.

I smirked at him. "Like what you feel?"

"Very, very much. I want to knead them like dough. You have an amazing ass. Always have," Noah admitted. "I remember watching you skate and cursing all of that fucking padding."

"You stared at my ass on the ice?"

He rolled his eyes at me. "I stared at your ass any chance I got. Everyone did."

I moved off him to lie on my back and pull him into my side. "Tell me."

"Well, you already know Henry Kenny had a massive crush on you. So he was front and center of the people who gawked. Then there was Jo Shepherd."

I laughed. "Jo must have asked me out twenty times before she finally gave up. It's like she didn't understand what gay meant."

"She still doesn't. You remember Timmy Andrews? Gay as the day is long, but Jo has tried to set him up with every single woman in her bridal party. Poor guy."

I brushed the hair out of Noah's face so I could see his eyes. "Wait, I thought Timmy was with John Paul Whatshisname?"

Noah looked up at me with a shit-eating grin. "No. JP ran off with Mr. Armstrong."

I thought about our old calculus teacher. "What? Are you fucking kidding?"

"No. Supposedly they've been screwing around since you guys were in school. Mr. Armstrong broke it off out of fear for his job, but the minute his retirement hit, he grabbed his boy toy and headed for Puerto Vallarta."

I couldn't help but laugh my ass off at the image. "Poor Tim. He and JP were together for like, what, six years? God. What a waste of time. To be with the wrong person for so many years must suck."

"Yeah. It does," he said quietly. I realized he'd been in a similar waste of time relationship, and I wondered if I should have apologized for what I'd said. He spoke up before I could. "Timmy was pretty wrecked, but he'll be fine. Better to find out now than ten more years from now."

I leaned over and pressed a kiss to his temple. "And, who knows? Maybe that experience will somehow lead him to where he's meant to end up."

Noah leaned his head back to gaze at me with those lovely green eyes that seemed to stare right into the deepest part of me.

"Maybe."

We did the staring thing again, and I started to feel myself losing control of the situation. I was having thoughts and feelings for him I had no business having. He wasn't even thirty yet, and he'd just gotten out of a serious relationship. He needed time and space to find himself, to party, to experience the freedom of being young, hot, and single in San Francisco.

The last thing he needed was a workaholic thirty-four-year-old whose most committed relationship was with his dry cleaner. Hooking up for fun and physical pleasure was one thing, but neither one of us was in a place to be considering anything more. I was married to the job and Noah was on the rebound.

"It's, ah, late. So... we should probably get some sleep," I said, moving to get up.

For the briefest moment, uncertainty flashed across his face. "Yeah, sure. You're right."

We both stood and collected our clothes from the floor. Noah looked around like he was unsure of which way to go, and I bit my tongue to keep from inviting him to my bed.

"See you tomorrow?" I said instead.

"Right," he said, clearing his throat. "Tomorrow."

I walked in the direction of my bedroom while he turned the opposite way. Despite knowing I was being awkward and weird, I couldn't help but turn back.

"Noah?"

"Yeah," he said with a resigned sigh that made my chest tight.

"I'm really looking forward to our date tomorrow night."

The smile on his face wasn't huge, but it was there.

13

NOAH

The following day was insane. It started off with what I'd thought was a lunch date with Dante and AJ Marian, but what had turned out to be some kind of bizarre visit to another planet—one on which lived a trio of little old ladies completely off their fucking rocker.

To be fair, Dante had tried to warn me. I'd gotten a call while waiting on a bench by the hostess stand of the restaurant. When I'd picked up, Dante had sounded frantic.

"Don't kill me," he'd said in a rush.

"Why would I kill you? If you're running late it's fin—"

"No, you don't understand. We can't be there, and now my Aunt Tilly and her friends are coming to take my place. Long story. Look, just smile and nod. Your goal is to get through it, Noah. Stand firm."

I heard static and mumbling through the phone before Dante came back.

"Sorry, Noah! Gotta go."

The call left me standing there dumbfounded until I heard a commotion behind me.

"There he is," the tall one, Irene, said with a sweet smile. "Hi, Noah."

I returned her smile and greeted all three of them. Irene's wife, who I'd only ever known as "Granny" was the oldest and tiniest of the three, and Dante's Aunt Tilly was the regal one looking down her nose at all of the peasants surrounding us in the cafe.

"Ladies, how are you?"

Granny approached and peered at me with one eye as if searching for defects in the skin of my face.

"Meh, you'll do." She shrugged and waved to the hostess for a table.

I glanced at Irene who was busy reaching for Granny's elbow to keep the little woman from escaping, no doubt.

That left Tilly.

"Don't worry, kid," she said. "We're here to help."

I was almost too afraid to ask. "Help with what?"

She didn't answer until we were seated side by side in a plush booth by a large window and the ladies had all ordered mimosas.

"We're going to find you a man," Tilly said with a satisfied grin. "Leave it to us. We're really good at this."

I stared at her for a beat. "Oh. No. No, thank you," I replied as politely as humanly possible. "Your nephews are already trying very hard to—"

"Poppycock," Granny said. "They're amateurs. Who has more life experience, Noah? Those whippersnappers or the three of us?"

I did the math, and the Marian men still won.

"You?" I said anyway. Obviously, it was what was expected of me.

"Damned straight," Tilly muttered from behind her menu.

Irene chimed in. "So, dear, we just need to ask you a few preliminary questions, if you don't mind."

Granny leaned across the table with a big grin while I took a sip of my ice water. "Pitcher or catcher?"

After a classic spit take, things got interesting.

"I'd prefer not to... ah... say." I tucked my napkin into my lap and pretended to study the menu.

Tilly narrowed her eyes at me. "You scream bottom, son."

I closed my eyes and counted to twenty. In Pig Latin.

"Can we please change the ubject-say?" I asked.

Irene snorted, and Granny looked around for someone. "Where's that skinny gal with the weird eyeball? I need a drink."

I gently slid her mimosa closer to her so she could see it. She eyed me suspiciously. "That's mine. Get your own."

"Yes, ma'am."

After ordering another round, Tilly turned to me with a big open smile. "Alright. Let's get started. If you had to sum up what you're looking for in one of these categories, which would it be? Bear, otter—"

"Please," I began. "I don't want to—"

"Hush," Granny interjected. "Doesn't matter anyway. Clearly he's a Daddy Chaser."

My mouth opened but no words came out.

Irene piped up. "Huh. I did not see that coming. Interesting."

"No," I croaked. "Not a... what was that again?"

"Tilly, get out your notes," Granny said, gesturing to a large purse by Tilly's elbow. "Maybe he's into puppy play or watersports."

Irene looked around the restaurant before leaning in and whispering. "I believe that's called a Puppy Pile. You know, when lots of pups and... ah... daddies get together for... play."

"No," I said again. I wasn't quite sure what to say to shut them up, but whatever words were needed, weren't happening.

"Oh, huh," Tilly said. "Maybe that's not his thing. What about whips and chains? A little PTSD?"

"BDSM," the young server suggested helpfully as she set a basket of rolls on the table. "And I'm going to go ahead and vote a no on that one for your cute friend here," she said, winking at me before scampering off to the luscious haven of the kitchen.

Granny threw up her hands, causing another server to narrowly avoid crashing to the floor with a giant tray of entrees. "Goddammit, then what the hell do you like in the sack, Noah?" she shouted.

The entire restaurant went silent.

"Um, a to-go order?" I whispered.

WHEN I'D BEEN THOROUGHLY INTERROGATED, FOUND lacking, coached, and re-interrogated with better results, the crazy trio declared our long lunch finally over.

"We'll be in touch," Tilly had assured me on the sidewalk out front of the restaurant.

"Ma'am?" I asked. "Like I said before, I don't really need help with—"

"Nonsense," she huffed.

Irene tried to come to my rescue. Sort of. "No sense in arguing, Noah. I promise you the two of them will get their way regardless. The best way to survive the riptide is to swim with it."

"It's cold as Santa's balls out here," Granny griped. "Where's the goddamned car?"

Tilly took one step to the open rear door of a dark town car and peeked in. "You still here?"

I saw a handsome older man step out of the open door in a full bespoke suit. His face registered calm patience. It was a familiar face. A politician or something I couldn't place. Surely he hadn't been sitting in this car waiting for her for the entire two-hour lunch we'd just had?

"Matilda," he said, stepping around and holding the car door open. "If you and your friends are done talking, I'll be happy to escort you all home now."

The woman herself sniffed at him and turned to enter the car. I heard her mumble something to him that sounded like *I'm tired*. The look on his face softened as he nodded and murmured a response. *Let's go home then, sweetheart.*

It was the smallest of exchanges, but it made my chest tight.

As I said my final goodbye to Granny, I leaned over to kiss her cheek. She patted mine in response before grinning at me.

"I snapped a selfie of you when you weren't looking. When we get home, I'll email you your Grindr login dealie. They got leather daddies on there to die for. Don't worry, kid, we'll pick you a good one."

And with a wink, they were off.

I really, really needed to meet some new people who weren't related in any way, shape, or form to the Marian family.

OF COURSE, I'd spent most of the rest of the day dreaming about Luke and our encounter on the sofa the night before. He'd sucked me off. Luke Holland had sucked my dick.

I'd gotten head from Luke goddamned Holland.

If I'd had a nice pair of cheerleading pompoms, I might have shaken them for a minute in private.

But then Luke had pulled the usual cool-guy routine and made it clear we were retiring into our separate corners.

Fuck that.

No, really. Fuck that.

I was determined. Tonight, we were not only going to sleep together, but we were also going to *sleep together.*

If he was going to keep doing this stupid-ass two-step of sexual feint and parry with me, I was going to have to bring in the big guns.

My backbone.

I pep-talked myself the entire way home from the alien lunch and was good and fired up by the time Luke came through the apartment door to get ready for our date.

"Strip," I said calmly but firmly.

He froze midway into peeling off his winter coat. "What?" he asked.

"Take all of your clothes off," I elaborated, standing from the kitchen stool and walking over to him.

"Why? What do you mean?"

"I mean, I want to have sex with you. Right now. I want to suck you off, and I want you to do the same to me. I don't particularly care *how* or *where*, but the *when* part... the *when* part is now."

As I spoke, his eyes darkened. He began to move, shucking the coat off, followed by the suit jacket and his shoes. Everything fell to the floor exactly where he removed it.

When Luke spoke, it was pure, deep sex rumble. "Then why aren't you naked already?" he asked.

I couldn't help but admit the truth while he stalked closer to me, stripping off clothes as he moved. I gulped. I wasn't quite sure I'd actually expected him to comply with my demands, so I began to babble.

"The maintenance man said he was stopping by at some point to check something, and I was afraid of being naked when he——"

Luke pounced. He grabbed me around the waist and crashed his lips into mine with a growl. I wanted to laugh from the very idea that I'd been the one controlling this scenario.

As if that was even in the realm of possibility between the two of us.

Every part of me wanted to beg him—to whimper the word *please* over and over again until he slid his thick cock into me and pounded me toward the world's greatest release.

But I didn't want to seem desperate.

"Please," I heard myself whimper like a child.

Motherfucker. Couldn't I withhold some dignity for even a minute? Just, like, a smidge?

"You're going to make me come without even taking your clothes off," Luke grumbled into my mouth. "Hearing you beg makes me fucking crazy, Noah."

"Please," I breathed again. Not because he liked it, but because I simply couldn't hold it in. I wanted him so much I could hardly keep from screaming in frustration.

"I want you naked on my bed. Now, Noah. Go," he said.

The cocksure attitude he was rocking sucked all of the blood flow well away from my brain, and I felt dizzy. Somehow I made it to his room, yanked off all my clothes and climbed onto his giant bed.

The place where Luke had all the sex.

Luke's sex bed.

Not that it intimidated me. Because it didn't. But, then again, the man he usually slept with in that bed was a goddamned Calvin Klein underwear model.

I felt my stomach drop at the reminder and lurched off the bed to reach for my clothes again. There was no fucking way I could let him see my body when I'd seen billboards all over town showing off what Luke was used to in bed. What had I been thinking?

I scrambled to put my pants back on but only managed to get one leg in before I heard his voice behind me.

"Noah?"

I tripped and fell over on the floor.

"Yeah?" I croaked.

He strode over to me with creased eyebrows. "You okay?"

Fuck, he was a sweetheart. God damnit.

"Maybe this wasn't such a good idea, Luke," I began.

The crease between his brows deepened. "Why not? What happened to change your mind?"

I looked anywhere but at him. "I'm not an underwear model."

Confusion morphed to understanding, and his entire demeanor changed.

"Thank god," he admitted in a light, conversational tone. He reached for my pants and began to pull them off me as if he was just helping me out of a pesky, uncomfortable pair of snow pants. "Those guys make me feel inadequate," he admitted. "And they're always ordering salads with no dressing and only ice water to drink. Ugh. Stresses me out."

He busied himself folding the pants and setting them on the floor before holding out his hand to help me up.

I stood and made my way to the bed while he continued to talk while stripping off his own clothes. He was talking in such an everyday way, I was hardly aware of my nakedness. Still, I slid under the covers as soon as I got to his bed.

He kept talking. "I once dated a guy who was so paranoid about his physique, he wouldn't let me go down on him unless he had that magical V shape showing on his stomach. If he'd had too much beer or salt and thought his abs weren't defined enough, he'd stay dressed and insist on sucking me off instead."

I felt a laugh bubble up. "And you're complaining about that?"

His eyes met mine, and I could see the seriousness there. "I like to give as much as receive, Noah. Maybe even more so."

Oh god.

I wondered idly if the apartment building had a portable AED machine just in case my heart actually stopped beating.

Luke went on. "And, anyway, he was a little too obsessed with feet. Kept asking me what size shoes and socks I wore and how often I trimmed my toenails. It was creepy."

As he continued babbling, I wondered if it was because of nerves. But suddenly I realized he was talking about nonsense to help *me* relax. Because *I* was the nervous one.

"Luke, I'm fine," I assured him. "Or I would be if you weren't talking about another man's toenails. Come over here."

His head came up from where he was stepping carefully out of his pants. His cock was ramrod straight against his lower belly, proving the inane chitchat hadn't been about any kind of reluctance or lack of interest on his part.

His body was magnificent. His long muscled legs were smattered in dark, masculine hair and the matching patch of curls surrounding his cock was neatly trimmed. For a brief moment, I pictured him alone in the bathroom with the electric trimmers and one of those shapely legs propped up somewhere. Heavy balls hung down and... *what the fuck was I doing fantasizing about Luke's naked body when the real goddamned thing was right there in front of me?*

I blinked and focused on the body coming toward me like a stalking panther—lean and sleek. His narrow hips were pale compared to the darker skin of his arms and it reminded me that I was one of the rare humans who was lucky enough to see that tender skin of his—the spots left covered even when he was wearing nothing more than a small bathing suit.

My mouth watered as I crawled forward toward the foot of the bed. "Want you in my mouth."

His face lit into a wide grin. "Feeling better?"

All I could see was his gorgeous fucking cock in front of me. "Uh-huh," I mumbled with a nod.

He stepped against the end of the bed just as I got to the edge and straightened up on my knees. Luke's hand came up to clasp the front of my throat in a gentle hold, forcing me to look at his eyes. His voice was soft but firm. "If you want to stop, we stop. If you want to do something different, just say the word. I don't ever want you to feel uncomfortable in my bed, Noah."

I just stared at him.

"Noah. Do you understand?"

"Uh-huh," I repeated dumbly.

His smile was the sexiest fucking thing I'd ever seen. It dripped seduction.

"Say it, Noah. Tell me you understand that you're in charge of what happens here."

"You're in charge of what happens here," I said obediently.

He snorted. "How can I have a serious conversation with you when you're so goddamned adorable?"

"I said what you wanted me to say," I replied in confusion as I replayed the words in my mind. Fuck. Okay, maybe I'd said it a little wrong. *Freudian slip.* The mistake made me blush. "I'm a big boy, Luke. Not a virgin."

His hand was still around the front of my throat, and the hold functioned like a dispenser button on my dick. Precum slid out in a steady dribble.

"Kiss me," I begged in a whisper. "Please."

He rewarded me with a soft press of his lips, one that I took complete advantage of by grasping the back of his head and pulling him in for a deeper one. Our tongues met and became one, twisting together naturally as if we'd already spent years learning each other's kiss.

My free hand reached for my own cock, but Luke stopped it before I could touch myself.

"No, baby," was all he said.

It was enough.

My hands moved around his waist to hold him for a minute before sneaking their way down to the tight curve of his ass. I squeezed, making him moan into my mouth, and I was pretty sure I felt the hand on my throat tighten just the smallest amount before releasing me altogether.

Finally, I could move from his grasp. I quickly moved my mouth down his throat, his chest, the defined plane of his abdomen, to the dark nest of curls I'd been drooling over earlier.

His cock was stiff and dark, jutting out toward me just waiting for my mouth. I took my time dropping light kisses along its length until I reached the sac below and began to pull his balls into my mouth one at a time.

Luke sucked in a breath and clutched at the hair on my head, murmuring encouraging phrases every time something felt particularly outstanding. It felt unbelievably good to be the one to make him lose control—to be the one who held his pleasure in my hands and could make the man whimper with just the barest touch of my tongue along his inner thigh.

"Noah." It wasn't a sigh, a sound of desire. It was a warning. One I instinctively knew meant to get on with the program before he decided to take control back.

I engulfed his hard cock in my mouth and sucked him down as far as I could, gagging on his length and loving the feel of the tears that sprung to my eyes. Something inside my gut knew seeing me gag on his cock would turn him on even more.

"Fuck," he growled. "Fuck, Noah."

I bobbed up and down shallowly again before taking him all the way into my throat and gagging again. Luke's grip in my hair tightened as he cried out. When I pulled off that time, his cock was covered in saliva, glistening strings still connecting him to my lips. I slowly looked up at him from under my lashes.

"*Jesusfuckingchrist*, turn around and get on your hands and knees," Luke ground out.

Yes, please, I thought.

14

LUKE

How could I think with his mouth on my cock? I couldn't.

My brain kept flipping back and forth between thinking Noah was cute as hell and hot as fuck. It didn't matter—either way, I needed to get inside him. It's all I could think about. I wanted to fuse our bodies together and hold tight to him for as long as I could.

While he scrambled around on the bed, I stepped to the side table to get out a condom and lube. I hadn't intended to have anal sex with him this soon, but it was happening. Like he'd said, he wasn't a virgin. He was almost thirty years old. Why did I keep treating him like he was a kid who didn't know what he was doing?

He turned his head to look at me, and I saw the tiniest of smiles on his lips.

"Brat," I muttered. "You're driving me crazy on purpose."

"It's working," he responded cheekily. "Now, get the lead out, old man. Show me what you got."

Before crawling back on the bed, I leaned in and cupped his face, turning him toward me for a kiss. It was sweeter than I'd planned and seemed to go on forever. I felt Noah's hands trail along my sides and realized he'd turned over onto his back at some point during the kiss, and I was lying over him, my elbows propped on the bed by his ears.

I pulled back to gaze at his face. His green eyes were bright, and his skin was flushed a gorgeous shade of pink. A few light freckles remained scattered over his nose, and I wondered briefly when he'd been in the sun last. When we were growing up, he'd gotten freckles in the summer sun, but they'd always disappeared in the winter gloom. I loved those damned things.

"You're beautiful, Noah," I told him. "So fucking beautiful."

His fingers came up to my face and traced the bottom edge of my lower lip before moving up to thread into my hair. "Thank you, Luke."

I landed soft kisses on his mouth again, and what had been a fevered sprint toward Fuckville became a languid dance toward someplace different. A place I wanted to explore with him. Just the two of us, and for longer than just tonight.

We moved together slowly but with complete commitment to pleasing each other the best way we knew how. Our cocks slid together while we kissed and arched into one another until neither one of us could stand not being inside of each other anymore.

"Please," Noah begged again. It was a sound, a word I'd never get tired of hearing out of his mouth.

The lube was cold on my fingers so I rubbed them together to warm it up as much as I could before sliding my hand below his balls to smear it against his tender skin. I felt his puckered entrance respond to my touch and couldn't help but want to see it too. I moved down on the bed, stopping for a quick but thorough suck of his cock on the way down.

Once I kissed my way even lower, I pushed his thighs back toward his chest. His hands landed on my head, and I felt gentle fingers fiddling with my hair, almost like he wanted to examine the texture of it.

I slid a finger into him and watched his entire body respond. His muscles quivered, his skin flushed, and his breaths came quicker. The sound of his pleading interspersed with hisses of pleasure as I added another finger and then another. Noah was so responsive; I couldn't help but search out his prostate, even knowing it might end the whole thing too soon.

He cried out and scrabbled for me with his hands, begging me to get on top of him and fuck him already.

As soon as I stretched out above him, he reached for my cock to give it a few strokes before presenting the condom with a huff of impatience. Once I was ready, I leaned forward and kissed him again and again as my cock began pushing into his body.

At first, he felt so tight I worried he'd lied to me. Worried he'd never had anal sex and just hadn't wanted to admit it. But then he'd grabbed my hips and yanked me closer while lifting his ass up toward me as much as he could. Our bodies slammed together, and I cried out.

"Fuck, fuck, you feel good, Noah... *Fuck.*"

"Oh god," he moaned. "Oh god, please. You're gonna make me come. I-I can't..."

I tried slowing down, but I couldn't. My body wanted to be deep inside of him, and my hips continued to propel themselves in and out as hard and fast as possible.

"Can't get enough," I groaned against his hot mouth. "*Fuck.*"

"Just like that," he cried, digging his nails into my ass.

I made a point of keeping the same angle and pegging his prostate as much as I could. His cock was bucking against my stomach, and I grabbed for it, tugging with slick fingers once, twice, until he arched his head back and his eyes rolled up into his head.

That was all I needed. As soon as he cried out his release, I let go —mindless shudders of my own climax rocking me from the inside out. Even after my orgasm ebbed, I stayed pressed into him, unwilling to back away and break the connection.

I dropped a kiss on the side of his neck and nuzzled my nose behind his ear. Noah's legs came around me and hooked together behind my back to hold me to him.

We were on the same page, neither of us ready to part.

Our bodies were slick with sweat and sticky with cum, but I didn't give a shit. I felt his solid heart thundering against mine and the warm puffs of his breath glancing along my damp shoulder. His fingers moved slowly through invisible designs on my back as we caught our breath.

"Baby, I need to pull out," I murmured against his ear. "Be right back, okay?"

He didn't say anything, but he let me go. I made my way quickly to the bathroom to clean up and bring a warm wet towel for him. As I returned to the bed, I was overcome with emotion out of the blue.

It was weird. Like... some kind of cross between extreme attraction, comfort, heat, protectiveness, possession, familiarity, and complete and utter *rightness*. It made my throat feel tight in a way it never had before.

I locked eyes with him and saw his gorgeous face looking soft and vulnerable.

Mine.

I swallowed the thought down and reached to help clean him off. My mouth itched to say other ridiculous words, but I swallowed those down too.

This wasn't what I'd wanted or what he'd needed. I wanted my usual, sex with no feelings. And Noah... Noah needed rebound sex. Light, and fun... no strings attached.

What the hell was happening between us? While it was certainly fun, that sure as hell hadn't felt light. And there had been strings tangled up everywhere inside of me eager to be connected to the man in my bed.

"Come on, beautiful. We need to get ready for that party," I said in an effort to lighten the mood from all of the crazy thoughts I was having. I wondered if he could see through my smile to the terror below.

~

WHEN WE ARRIVED at the restaurant to have dinner with Ginger and Pete before the party, I finally took a good look at Noah. He was dressed in a dark suit and looked amazing. The soft lighting of the steakhouse made strands of his brown hair appear golden, and I noticed more than a few people turn their heads to look at him. He fidgeted with his cuffs and kept his eyes downcast, so I reached over to take his hand in mine.

"You're the most beautiful person in this room," I murmured low enough so he was the only one to hear it.

The compliment seemed to make him even more self-conscious, which certainly hadn't been my intention. I tried chatting about nonsense to put him at ease, telling him about Pete and Ginger's three kids.

"Chloe and Hazel are gorgeous and couldn't be more different. I'm sure you'll meet them at some point over the holidays. Then there's the baby, Tommy. Most spoiled little brother ever. Gets all the attention from the entire extended family. Reminds me of a certain someone I know," I said, squeezing his hand.

Noah smiled and blushed, which did things to my stomach. I considered whether I should still be holding his hands when our friends arrived, but I couldn't seem to let him go. Before I knew it, they were there and the hostess was seating us in a dark booth along one wall. Whatever nerves Noah had about the evening seemed to melt away once he saw Ginger.

"Sorry we're late," Pete began before Ginger cut in.

"Someone takes way too long to fix his precious head of hair," she said, throwing a not-so-subtle head tilt toward her husband. Pete's eyes rolled up and Noah laughed.

"That right, Pete?" I asked. "Trying to maximize coverage now that it's thinning in your old age?"

Peter Marian had the thickest head of hair of anyone I knew. He'd go to his grave with enough for ten men. Regardless, his hand came up to pat it as if to make sure it was all still there. Ginger winked at Noah before turning her attention on our server to order drinks.

Once we were all settled with some nice wine and a table full of appetizers, the conversation was in full swing. Being with Pete and Ginger had always been easy, but being with the two of them and

Noah... it was like sliding into a warm bath on a cold night. Relaxing, comforting, and even indulgent in a way.

"So, Noah, how's the licensing process going?" Ginger asked. "Dante told us you have a job lined up in the emergency room and are just waiting for your nursing license to transfer."

"I've done everything I need to do. Now it's just a matter of waiting for them to process it. I went down to the hospital the other day to update some information in the human resources department and met one of the doctors I'll be working with. Everyone there is so nice; I'm looking forward to starting."

Pete put his arm around his wife's shoulder. "My brother Thad's fiancée is a doctor in that hospital. By any chance have you met Sarah Alexander yet?"

"No, the doctor I met was Ethan Rhodes. But I've also met several of the nurses."

Ginger smiled over her wineglass. "We'll make sure you meet Sarah when you come to the vineyard for Christmas."

Noah looked down at his lap for a moment, seeming unsure. "I know you all said I was welcome, but Christmas is usually a family thing and..."

Ginger's eyes narrowed. *Uh-oh.* I placed my hand on Noah's leg without thinking.

"Don't even think about backing out, Noah," Ginger said in her maternal voice. "You'll be there. Everyone's counting on it."

"Yes, ma'am," he said with a nervous chuckle. "You remind me of Pete's Aunt Tilly. She kind of scares me a little."

I looked at him in surprise. "You've met Tilly?"

"If by 'met' you mean 'got trampled by,' then yes, I've met Tilly. She and her homegirls ambushed me yesterday. I have Dante to thank for that."

"Shit," Pete said with a snort. "Oh god."

Ginger looked tickled. "Classic. What did they say?"

"It was a blur, really. I'm pretty sure it was about setting me up on Grindr? Does that sound like something that could have happened?"

Pete and Ginger laughed too hard to answer, but I turned to him.

"Yes. It for sure happened, but no. You're not going out on a Grindr hookup."

Noah's eyes widened. "Why not? Everyone uses Grindr. Why not me too?"

I'd never felt so annoyed with a trio of old ladies in my life. "Because. That's why," I managed to say without making a fool out of myself.

For some reason that only made Pete and Ginger laugh more.

"What?" I asked. "Don't tell me you think Noah should be hooking up with random dudes around the city."

"No, certainly not," Ginger agreed. "In fact, Luke, we think *you* should be the only person he dates from here on out."

Pete nodded his head in enthusiastic agreement.

Noah and I sat there staring at the two of them through the haze of awkward between us.

"I'm sorry, what?" Noah asked weakly. I was learning it was his go-to stalling technique.

"I agree," I coughed. "Just safer that way."

I thought Pete Marian's eyes were going to bug right out of his face. Instead, they locked onto mine with the promise of a serious talk the next time he got me alone.

"Can we change the subject?" I asked. "How're the girls doing?"

Thankfully, the rest of dinner passed in enjoyable companionship. By the time we arrived at the firm's holiday party in a downtown hotel ballroom, all four of us were significantly bubbly and giddy from the several bottles of wine we'd shared at the restaurant.

I didn't even realize I was holding Noah's hand again until he slid his out of mine when we walked into the ballroom. I looked over at him in confusion.

"You probably don't want people to think we're together," he murmured.

I reached for his hand again and let out a breath once I felt its now-familiar warmth in mine. "You're probably wrong."

His smile was as golden as he was. Breathtaking and all encompassing. I found myself leaning forward to kiss those grinning lips when I heard someone call my name.

"Luke, care to introduce us to your friend?"

I turned to see a guy named Isaac from the trusts-and-estates department. Despite being a top-producing attorney in the firm, the guy got on my last nerve. He always asked me nosy questions about my love life and had seemed downright giddy when he'd run into Victor and me at a club one night several weeks before.

"Isaac, this is Noah Campbell. Noah, Isaac Brandt. He's an attorney specializing in wealth management," I said in an effort to be polite.

Noah held his free hand out for a shake. I saw Isaac's eyes fixate on where I held Noah's hand before he looked up at me with a knowing wink, taking Noah's outstretched hand with both of his own. Despite the creepy handshake with Noah, Isaac's eyes were on me.

"Where's Victor tonight?"

"No idea. Please excuse us, Isaac. Jasmine is trying to get my attention." Without waiting for a response, I led Noah to a bar area on the far side of the room where Jasmine and her man, Davi, were in line for drinks. When she saw the two of us approaching, her face lit up.

"There you are. I thought maybe you'd gotten caught up at the office after I left to get my hair done," she said before turning to Noah. "You must be Noah; it's so nice to meet you. Luke talks about you all the time."

Jesus, I was going to have to kill her.

Noah's eyes glanced to mine with a smirk. "Is that right? I'd love to know what he's told you."

"Nothing, she's being a pain in the ass as usual. Ignore her," I said.

After I greeted Davi and introduced him to Noah, the four of us got our drinks and made our way to a table.

Jasmine sat beside Noah and leaned in to confide something to him. "So, Noah, Luke has told me all about your crazy job..."

15

NOAH

My stomach dropped. Luke told his assistant that I sold Love Junk? I shot him a look that caused the smile to freeze on his face. He tilted his head in confusion.

"Um..." I said, trying like hell to think of a way out of the topic. We were at Luke's fancy law firm holiday party in one of the swankiest hotels in the city. What the hell would happen if his other coworkers learned I sold—

"Being an ER nurse must be so interesting," she continued. "I've always wondered about the stories you guys must have."

I blinked at her as the reality of what she was asking sank in. I glanced at Luke and saw concern etched on his face. He'd only told her about my job as a nurse. That was what she was asking about.

After grabbing for his hand again and squeezing it in unspoken apology, I turned back to Jasmine. "It is. I love it. Every shift is something new. New people to treat, new families to help. It's amazing to know what you do makes a difference, and it's even more amazing to watch what doctors are able to accomplish to put people back together again."

Jasmine's face beamed up at me. "That's lovely, Noah."

"Well, I have to admit... I miss it. I wish this license process didn't take so long."

Davi leaned in to speak. "What are you doing with yourself in the meantime?"

I glanced at Luke, assuming he'd be embarrassed by my Love Junk gig. Instead, he winked at me and responded before I could.

"Spending as much time with me as possible, if I can help it. But when he's not doing that, he has a temporary sales job. He's got that gig *licked* too. It's *hard* but very *satisfying*. Brings his clients lots of *pleasure*."

I choked on my drink and began coughing up a lung. Luke patted me on the back a few times before running that hand up into the hair on the nape of my neck and leaning in to drop a kiss on the side of my face.

"Sorry, couldn't help myself," he chuckled softly in my ear.

"Beware the revenge, Lucas," I warned trying not to shudder at the brief brush of his lips on the edge of my ear. "It will be swift and harsh."

"Baby, when I'm with you, I promise nothing will be swift *or* harsh," he said so only I could hear.

Oh god.

"Um, where's the restroom?" I croaked. Jasmine shot me a smirk before pointing me in the right direction. I pushed back from the table and made sure to close my suit jacket quickly in order to hide my adolescent dick.

When I got to the men's room, I hid away in a closed stall so I could catch my breath and calm down. Luke had implied wanting to spend lots of time with me, which made me feel like maybe this really was what I hoped for—the start of something real. I felt my lips curve into a smile as I contemplated that I was dating Luke Holland.

Finally.

I wasn't just another one-night-stand or fuck buddy. Was I? Wait. Maybe he meant he wanted to spend lots of time with me *fucking*. But surely, I was more important to Luke than a quick lay, right?

I blew out a breath of frustration at the fact I even cared about shit like that. Why couldn't I be like a normal man my age and just look forward to the fucking without worrying about relationship bullshit?

Just before I reached for the stall door, I overheard two men come in laughing and talking. The sound of Luke's name hit my ears.

"Luke's date is cute as fuck," the first man said. I felt my face warm in surprise at the compliment.

"Gio, you're crazy if you think you have a chance with one of Luke's boys. Remember when you flirted with Whit, that guy Luke brought to the park last summer? Shot you down with one look."

"Yeah, in front of Luke. Then I had that dude screaming my name the following weekend out at the club," the man said with a laugh. "He told me Luke's the type to fuck and forget."

"Still. Maybe don't make your move on that guy until after Luke's done with him, okay?"

They continued chuckling through washing their hands and leaving the bathroom. I stood frozen long after they were gone. My stomach felt like a cauldron of acid and all of the joy of my earlier sexual encounter with Luke fell into the acid with a sharp hiss.

Surely when they said Luke liked to fuck and forget, that didn't mean me?

On the way back to the ballroom from the men's room, I ran into Luke's coworker Isaac.

"Noah, there you are. I was hoping to talk to you if I could get you away from Luke long enough," he said with a friendly smile.

"Uh, okay."

"I haven't met you before. Are you new in town?" he asked as he gestured me forward into the ballroom.

"Yes. I moved here from Canada a few weeks ago." I followed him blindly, still reeling from what I'd heard in the bathroom.

"How do you know Luke?"

Isaac walked to the nearest bar, and I followed him since we were in the middle of a conversation.

"We grew up together," I explained. "So when I decided to move here, he offered to show me around."

"And the two of you are..." His expression was more than curious, and I began to feel uncomfortable.

"The two of us are...?" I responded. Part of me wanted to be polite, but I couldn't help but point out how rude his leading question had been. "Men. Professionals. Canadian. Hockey fans. Wearing suits..."

He laughed. "Sorry, I meant are the two of you sleeping together?"

My eyebrows might have impaled themselves into my hairline. "I don't see how that's any of your business. And I'm not sure Luke would appreciate me talking about him behind his back to a coworker either. Please excuse me."

I turned to make my way back to the man himself when Isaac reached out and clasped my arm. "Wait, Noah. I'm sorry. You're right. That was rude. Just please give me a second."

The last thing I wanted to do was embarrass Luke at his work event. I didn't know who this Isaac really was to him, so I needed to keep my cool. After swallowing my frustration and making sure my polite mask was back in place, I faced him again.

Isaac sighed. "I apologize. I guess that was a little jealousy coming out. Luke has the ability to always draw the attention of the hottest guy in the room, and it makes me feel like I'm running to catch up."

What a douche. "It's not a competition, Isaac."

"Wrong. With Luke, it is. He collects gorgeous men like trophies. Never keeps any of them."

My heart clenched in my chest as I tried to keep his words from hitting their mark. Too late. I knew he was right. After all, Isaac wasn't even the first person *tonight* to say so.

I blew out a breath of resignation. "What's your point?"

"I'd like to take you to dinner."

I almost snorted despite my heavy heart. "No, thanks."

"Please. At least meet me for coffee. I can wait until the fling with Luke is over. I can tell you're someone special, Noah."

That was even more laughable than him asking me out after his rude diatribe. Before I had a chance to reject him again, I felt a large hand on the small of my back.

"You okay?" I heard in my ear. For some reason, my eyes stung even as I tried my hardest to harden myself against the feelings I was having toward Luke.

"Yes," I lied, turning toward him. "I was just getting ready to explain to Isaac that I'd moved in with you."

Isaac's jaw dropped in surprise as Luke's eyebrows raised. I was nothing if not loyal. If Isaac thought he was in competition with Luke over my attentions, he needed to know it wasn't now, nor would it ever be, a question. I was Luke's, whether he wanted me to be or not.

Unfortunately, as I replayed my own words in my head, I realized how petty I'd sounded. Would Luke let me get away with implying we were living together as partners?

I felt my face flush with regret, fully expecting Luke to laugh it off.

Luke's voice was husky and deep. "And did you tell him that I had to order a new bed today to meet your specifications for certain... ideas you have?"

Oh thank god. The man knew how to play along.

"No. I thought that was just between us," I said, tucking my face into his neck as if embarrassed. In reality, it was just an excuse to smell him and take comfort in his embrace for a brief moment.

Luke's arms slid around me and held me tight.

"That's giving me ideas, Noah," he growled. "I think it's time for me to take you home. Please excuse us, Isaac."

I didn't remember much of how we got home. Luke led me to a town car and proceeded to nibble warm, damp kisses along my neck and face until I was so dizzy with lust I could barely see straight.

If Luke was going to fuck and forget me, I was damned sure going to make the most of the fucking part.

We stumbled into the apartment with suit jackets and ties askew, both coats in a woolen ball under Luke's arm and beard burn covering my entire face.

"Wait, wait," I gasped, shoving him off me. I didn't want to—lord knew I didn't. But I needed to ask him if Isaac had been right. If what was happening between us was just some kind of game. If he saw me the same way he saw Victor. Friends with benefits.

Luke's eyes met mine with a pinch of concern between them.

"What's wrong? You want to slow down? Was I going too fast? Tell me."

After we shucked off our suit jackets and shoes, I led him to the sofa and turned to face him as we sat down next to each other. I noticed Luke's pinky finger was touching against the side of my thigh as if he just wanted to keep the simplest of physical connection going between us.

It took me a moment to gather my nerve. "Am I... I mean, is this..." I gestured between us. "Are we just... friends with benefits now?"

My face couldn't have been redder, but I soldiered on.

"Because part of me wants to say that's fine, you know? I'd love to take time with you any way I can get it. But, honestly, I think that might break me. Being with you one night and then watching you bring home someone else—"

"No," he said firmly. "I would never do that to you."

"Then what..." I took another minute to just breathe. "What is this?"

I knew I was taking a risk just by asking him that. I risked him rolling his eyes and throwing up his hands as if I was too high maintenance for him.

"Honestly, Noah, I don't know. But I know I enjoy being with you very much. Introducing you to my friends and coworkers was nice. I thought it would be weird since I'd never brought anyone I cared about to a work function before, but it was really fun."

"You haven't? But Ginger told me you'd brought Victor."

His eyes bore into mine as I realized what it meant. "You didn't care about Victor," I said softly.

Luke shook his head. "No."

"But you care about me?"

"Yes."

I could see the truth of it in his eyes, but I could also see fear. Like, maybe he hadn't meant to admit it or hadn't even realized it himself until that moment.

My face split into a wide grin. "Okay."

"Okay? What do you mean, okay?"

"I just wanted to make sure I wasn't one of your trophies like Isaac said."

His face turned from concerned and hesitant to downright homicidal.

"What the fuck did that guy say to you, Noah?"

"It doesn't matter," I said, shifting to crawl into his lap and cup his face with my hands.

"It matters to me," he bit out through clenched teeth. "Did he make you feel uncomfortable? I knew something was going on between you two. Your hackles were up."

I took his hand and put it on the bulge in my suit pants. "And now something else is up, so can we drop it and focus on more fun things, please?"

He groaned and leaned his head back onto the sofa cushion, eyes half-lidded and focused on me. "You've been driving me crazy all night, Noah. Wanted to have my hands all over you."

I unbuttoned my shirt slowly, enjoying the slight shifting in Luke's trousers beneath me. His eyes were riveted on my fingers as they pushed each button slowly through the holes. When I got to my waistband, I pulled the shirttail out of my pants and stripped the rest of the shirt off, followed quickly by my undershirt.

Luke's hands came up to caress my stomach and chest.

"So sexy," he murmured as his trailing fingers raised goosebumps across my skin. "So perfect."

His eyes moved up to watch my face as he lifted his hand to trace the contours of my collarbone. "Come to bed with me, Noah."

It wasn't a question.

My throat was too thick to respond verbally, so I just nodded and climbed off him.

Once we were in the bedroom, Luke took over.

He led me into his large master bathroom and started the shower. After turning several knobs, jets began to spray from every flat surface of the large space, and steam swirled around us. Luke's eyes never left my body.

He opened my pants and slid them off me, quickly returning his hands up the back of my thighs to do the same to my briefs. He made sure to slow the slide down over the bump of my ass cheeks and leaned in to drop kisses on my stomach as he did so.

My fingers brushed into his dark, wavy hair, and I smiled down at him. I thought about how a man could get used to seeing Luke Holland on his knees like that.

Once I was completely bare, he nudged me into the tiled shower stall and removed his own clothes methodically but quickly.

When he joined me in the shower, he immediately lowered to his knees again and began sucking me off.

Luke on his knees was a thing of beauty. I, on the other hand, was a wreck. My legs trembled and my breath caught as his mouth did things to me that made my mind go to another place. I was sobbing my need into the small chamber until he swiftly turned me and bent me over so he could treat my ass to the same oral attentions he'd given my cock.

Every nerve ending sparked and my leg muscles wobbled in response.

"Luke," I whimpered. "I can't... I can't..." I began to slide down onto the tiled floor. My legs just couldn't hold on any longer. My entire body was a wet noodle strung out in the very best way.

"I've got you, baby," he said with a deep chuckle. "It's okay. I can reach what I want just as easily with you on the floor."

I knew he was teasing me, but it was done with affection. His hands smoothed reverently over my body until I was too far gone to realize he'd gone from pleasuring me to washing me.

The man was thorough.

Fingers spread my ass to rub slick soap across my hole, and I clenched in response.

"Fuck me, please," I asked politely.

He chuckled again. "Don't worry. I'm going to."

"No, I mean *now*. Right now. Right this minute," I insisted in a weak voice. "Have to."

"I will."

"Right now," I said again.

"Yes, Noah."

"Promise me." I was babbling. I seriously couldn't think straight with his hands on me and what had to be fifteen-hundred spouts of warm water bathing me in relaxation. "Need it. Need you."

His finger had wiggled into my ass while his other hand finished washing me. I gasped as he hit my prostate, and I arched against him in search of another stroke like that.

"Beautiful, Noah," he said, tossing the soap away and pulling his finger out to gather me up in his arms. He stepped out of the shower and stood me up on the thick bath mat before drying me off with a plush towel from a warming rack.

"Even your towels feel like heaven," I mumbled, looking down as he ruffled the towel through my wet hair. I noticed my cock, angry and purple, jutting out toward him. "It's so mad at you," I observed.

"What is?" he asked, lifting a brow at me. He followed my gaze and saw my erection. His eyes darkened but his mouth quirked up. "Oh, that. Well, it'll have to wait."

"What?" I squawked, looking up. "Why? You promised." Fuck if I didn't sound like a petulant goddamned child, but the blood flow situation in my hindbrain was desperate and harkening me back to Neanderthal times. Caveman times. Honestly, I just couldn't fucking think.

He leaned down and threw me over his shoulder, walking the short distance to his large bed before depositing me in the center of it.

"I did promise. And I intend to deliver. But first I want to kiss your sweet mouth."

Smooth-talking goddamned sweetheart.

"Mm-hmm," I purred, lifting my chin to make it easier for him to reach my mouth. He climbed up and settled on top of me.

We kissed for hours or minutes or days. My skin was already sensitive with beard burn, but I didn't fucking care. I wanted him so badly.

My legs wrapped around his body and I arched my cock up into his stomach. "So help me god, Luke, if you make me keep begging, I'm going to give up."

He released the earlobe he'd been sucking and glanced at me. "No, you aren't."

No, I wasn't.

Finally, fucking *finally*, he was ready to enter my body. He'd teased me with his mouth, his fingers, and a crap-ton of dirty talk before he was finally ready to slide his cock into me.

I felt happily lightheaded with relief and giddy about the upcoming fuck fest.

Until he slid home and our eyes met.

Oh god. This was no fuck fest.

In Luke's eyes I saw it all. The desire, the fear, the desperation, the confusion.

And most unexpectedly, *proof.*

Proof I wasn't the only one falling.

16

LUKE

When my phone trilled in the wee hours of the morning, I felt groggy but good. My entire body felt used and sated. As I shifted to answer it, I felt the comforting press of Noah's warm body in front of mine. My knees were locked behind his and he cradled my hand against his chest.

I'd spent hours the night before worshipping his body and doing everything in my power to make him feel good. I wanted him to feel like the most adored man on the planet, and I poured all the new feelings I was having into our lovemaking. After he'd expressed his insecurities to me about being just another friends with benefits, I'd tried my hardest to show him how far that was from who he was to me.

The phone rang again and Noah let out an *mmpfh* as he turned his face into the pillow. I reached for the phone on my side table and saw it was Noah's brother. I also saw that the phone's clock said it was after three in the morning.

Fuck.

"Scott?" I answered in a rough voice. "You okay?"

Noah turned to me with a confused squint before sitting up.

"Yeah, man. We're outside the apartment. Can you come let us in?" Scott's voice was loud enough that Noah could hear it. The panic on his face was clear as day as he scrambled back and fell off the bed onto his ass.

"What?" I asked. "You're *here*? In San Francisco? Who's *we*?"

"Dude, it's the middle of the night. Our flights were delayed out the ass. Are you home? Can we talk about this inside?"

"Yeah—ah, yes. Hang on. Be right there."

I disconnected the call and stood, unsure of what the hell was happening.

"What the fuck?" Noah hissed.

"No idea. Calm down. Are you okay?"

"No. Fuck no. Who's with him?"

I looked around for some clothes to put on and found a pair of sweats folded on my dresser. Instead of slipping them on, I threw them at Noah. "Put these on. You can't exactly put back on your suit."

After rifling through my dresser for another set of clothes, I found some trackpants and a long-sleeved T-shirt.

Noah stood at the door to my bedroom pale as a sheet. "What are we going to tell him?"

My heart was already racing, but the idea of telling Scott I was fucking his baby brother was enough to send it tripping into the stratosphere. Scott was a giant of a man—an airplane mechanic in the air force and the kind of guy you'd never want to meet alone in a dark alley. Scott and Noah were like night and day.

"Nothing. We're not telling him anything, Noah, Jesus," I snapped. The instant I saw hurt flash across his face, I regretted it. "Noah, wait."

Too late. He'd already turned and stormed out of my room.

I tried taking some deep breaths to calm myself, wondering why Scott had flown all the way from Cold Lake to visit. Was he worried about Noah? Had something happened? Suddenly, I feared he was going to bring news that would hurt Noah. Was there any way I could stop it?

As I approached the apartment door, I saw Noah disappear around the corner of the kitchen toward the coffee maker. He was probably going to make tea and offer it to everyone the way he always did when he was unsure of what to do.

I took a final deep breath and opened the door.

There, next to Scott, was Gordon fucking Ewing—Noah's ex-boyfriend.

This was going to be a shitshow. Noah was going to flip out and try to make everything right for everyone. Which was impossible, of course.

"Uh, hey," I said, stepping forward to give Scott a brief hug and pat on the back. I ground my back teeth as I offered a handshake to Gordon. "Gordon, good to see you again," I lied. "Come on in."

They wheeled suitcases behind them and made their way into the room, shucking off parkas and kicking off their boots. Noah came around the corner quickly but skidded to a stop when he saw Gordon.

"Gord," he said in shock. "What... what..."

"Bug, thank god. You're a sight for sore eyes," he said, rushing over and scooping Noah up into his burly arms. The guy was built like Scott, not quite as wide maybe but tall and muscular. He made Noah look like a toy by comparison. I wanted to scream, whimper, cry, or... shoot something.

He was touching Noah. *My* Noah.

Fuck.

"What are you guys doing here?" I blurted, trying so fucking hard to rein in my shit.

Noah scrambled back out of Gordon's embrace, face blooming pink and eyes flitting everywhere, but mostly at me. I tried to somehow let him know it was okay. Whatever he needed to do or say or be would be okay with me. I just didn't want to see him upset.

"I came to bring Noah home, but it's kind of late," Gordon said to all of us. "Doodlebug, where's your room? I'm beat."

Noah's panicked eyes shot to mine. I wanted to tell Gordon where he could shove it— that Noah would be sleeping in my room, with me. But it wasn't my call. I wasn't the boss of Noah, and now that he was faced with his ex, there was no telling how he was really feeling.

Maybe after being with me, he realized how good he'd had it with Gordon.

Bullshit. I knew it was a load of crap the minute my mind went there.

But I still couldn't claim ownership of Noah, and three in the morning was not the time to open up the can of worms that Noah and I were sleeping together.

"Gordon, you can have my room," I offered instead. "And Scott can share with Noah. I'll be happy to sleep on the sofa."

Noah's eyes closed in relief, and I felt a swell of emotion tighten in my chest.

Just as Gordon began to argue, I noticed Scott recognize the panicked look on Noah's face. "Yeah, Gord. That's a good idea. I wanted to catch up with Noah anyway, and we can all regroup in the morning. Sure you don't mind, Luke?"

I swallowed my sigh of relief. "Course not. Let me just change the sheets really quickly."

Gordon patted me hard on the back. "Luke, it's the middle of the night. No need for fuss. I'll be fine."

I thought of Gordon sleeping on the sheets still warm with Noah's scent. Gord could burn in hell before I'd let him have that comfort tonight.

"I insist," I said at the same time Noah chimed in.

"Let him, Gord."

There was an awkward silence before Noah forced a laugh and began making shit up. "Luke's weird about cleanliness. When I first moved in, he insisted on washing the curtains before I could move my stuff in my room. Strange, right? And don't even get me started on the—"

I interrupted. "Does anyone want tea?"

AN HOUR later I was on the sofa under a stack of blankets feeling sorry for myself. The room was dark, and the three other men staying with me had long since quieted down in their respective corners of the apartment.

I thought about how happy Gordon had been to see Noah. Of course he'd been happy to see him. Who wouldn't be? Noah was everything a man could want in a boyfriend—handsome, smart, sweet, kind. He was thoughtful and giving, social and well liked. It was a privilege to know him and a joy to spend time in his company.

I knew the two of them had been together for several years, and I couldn't discount the importance of their shared history. There was no way I could compete with that. And if I stuck around making moony eyes at Noah, he'd never be able to focus his full attention on figuring out what he wanted to do about Gordon. Regardless of whether Noah and I ever had a chance together, he needed closure with Gordon first.

My stomach rolled with confusion and indecision. There was a massive chasm between what I wanted to do and what I knew I *should* do. After several more minutes of tossing and turning, I made up my mind. I stood up and folded the comforter, neatly stacking it on top of the pillow and making my way over to the overnight bag I'd packed so I wouldn't have to wake Gordon in the morning before work. My plan had been to go to the gym and then shower and get ready for work there, but now I had a different destination in mind.

I needed to give Noah some space. There was no way I could live with myself if I got in the way of what he wanted, and I knew he'd have a hard time being honest with me if he thought it would hurt my feelings.

After leaving a note for him on the kitchen counter, I snuck out the door.

A couple of hours later, I pulled up to the Alexander Vineyard right as Friday's daybreak warmed the naked vines with rosy morning light. I'd called ahead and gotten the night-shift worker at the front desk of the lodge. Luckily, there was a room ready for me when I arrived, and after emailing Jasmine and Pete about taking the day off, I climbed into bed.

17

NOAH

The minute Gordon and my brother had shown up at the apartment, I'd known I'd lost Luke. He'd looked freaked out, annoyed, and frustrated—put upon even.

He hadn't claimed me, hadn't reached out and taken my hand or stood up for me when Gord had said he wanted to take me home.

Luke hadn't fought for me at all.

And why should he have? We'd been together for all of five minutes. He didn't owe me anything. But fuck if I didn't want him to want me that way.

I'd slipped into a kind of numbness then—faced with not wanting the man who was there to fight for me and desperately wanting the man who seemed ambivalent about me.

Once I'd gone back to my room with Scott and settled into bed to sleep, I'd realized my assessment had been hasty. Maybe I'd misinterpreted Luke's response and he really was upset on my behalf. Maybe his annoyance hadn't been aimed at me too, just at Scott and Gordon.

But when I hadn't been able to get back to sleep, I'd snuck out to the living room to see him.

And found an empty sofa and a note on the kitchen counter.

Noah,

I'm heading out of town for the weekend to give your family some space. If you need anything, call Jasmine.

Luke

LUKE HAD RUN AWAY. Bolted at the first sign of trouble. If I hadn't been so goddamned heartbroken, I might have gotten angry.

I'd already told him, *told him*, I couldn't do this dance again. I couldn't handle him giving me his affection one minute and ripping it away the next.

But he'd fucking done it anyway.

I may not have been a fast learner, but I was catching on. If Luke Holland was going to bolt at the first sign of trouble, then he wasn't someone I could be with long term. Not that he'd even implied long term was possible or anything. Even wishing for long term with Luke made me feel like a child.

The men at the law firm holiday party were right. Luke wasn't relationship material.

Hadn't he tried to tell me? Hadn't he tried to warn me he didn't do relationships? Then why couldn't I have gotten that message through my thick fucking head? And why was I still hanging around waiting for him to change?

I'd felt every bit of the small-town kid right about then—pining after the gorgeous, successful attorney everyone wanted. I might as well have been doodling his name in my fucking notebook for how I felt about him then. The last thing a man like Luke needed was a little puppy trailing along panting after him.

I was an idiot.

When I'd dragged my ass back to bed, it was with my tail between my legs.

The following morning I was woken up with sloppy kisses to my neck. My gut knew right away something was wrong. The feeling was wrong; the smell was wrong. It was familiar but wrong. It wasn't Luke.

"What the hell?" I mumbled, scrambling away from Gordon. "Please don't."

His face registered surprise and hurt. Part of me, the part that was always polite to a T, wanted to apologize and make it up to him. But I resisted.

"Why are you in here?" I asked, looking around the room. "Where's Scott?"

"He went to pick up bagels, I think. Said he remembers a place nearby from when he visited before." He sat down on the bed next to me and leaned back against the headboard. "Are we going to talk about this? I want you to come home."

I had to admit the way he phrased it made it ten times easier on me. Had he asked how to fix things between us, or told me how much he loved me, or offered to move to California, things might have been harder. I might have somehow felt obligated to give him another chance, like somehow I owed him because we'd been together so long.

But asking me to give up San Francisco and go back to Cold Lake? No way.

"No, Gord. This is my home now. I'm happy," I tried to explain. Before I could even get to the part about our relationship being over for good, he interrupted.

"No, it isn't. Cold Lake is your home. Always has been. You belong there, Noah. With me." His large hands came up to cup the back of my head, but I pulled away.

"I overheard you one night at Bodean's," I blurted. "You were telling the guys things about me. Personal things."

Gordon looked confused for a moment until the memory came to him. An expression of relief washed across his face.

"Doodlebug, that was a joke. I was just talking shit with the guys. You know how it is."

The humiliating memory of the crass words he'd used came back to me and left me feeling small again.

"No. No one jokes like that about the person they love, says those words about the person they love," I said. "It's over, Gord. Go home."

He looked surprised for a moment until his expression turned apologetic. "I'm sorry, Bug. I really am. I didn't mean to make you feel bad about yourself. I love the things you do for me. I love the way you take care of me. I love *you*."

And that was just it. I knew he meant it. Of course he did. Who wouldn't love being cooked for and cleaned up after and given oral sex at the drop of a hat? But relationships weren't a one-way street, and I was through letting someone take without giving.

I moved to the opposite side of the bed and stood. "Gordon, when you find someone you truly do love, I hope that you'll consider cooking for them every once in a while. Or cleaning up after them when they're exhausted from an overnight shift. Or laying them down on the bed and worshipping their body with your mouth even if that night their lips never go near your own skin. What we had was nice, Gordon, and I loved living with you and playing house at first. But now I'm exactly where I'm meant to be. And I'm moving on."

He seemed to be considering my words, and I knew I had only moments left before he'd try again to convince me to go back to Cold Lake with him. I needed to get out of there.

I grabbed my clothes and shoved them into my messenger bag before striding out into the apartment to find my running shoes by the coatrack. Once I slipped them on and grabbed my coat, I made my way out of the apartment. Thankfully, I'd slept in the sweats Luke had tossed me hours before.

As I bolted out of the elevator into the lobby of the building, I ran into my brother.

"Scott," I said in surprise, lurching to a stop. He had a large brown paper grocery bag in one arm and a tray of fancy coffees in another.

"Where are you going? I picked up bagels and coffee for us."

"Why the hell did you bring him here, Scott?" I asked, cutting to the chase. "I left him."

"Why? Rose said he's been inconsolable, and you won't even answer his calls and explain what happened."

I gritted my teeth. "I left him a note. And the reason why is between the two of us."

Scott moved over to a nearby accent table to set the drink tray down. "Noah, talk to me. Mom and Dad are upset you bailed. I've run into two of your old coworkers who complained about missing you at work, and Rose and Gord's parents are even asking after you. What happened?"

"It's nothing huge, Scott. I just thought it was enough, and it wasn't."

"Cold Lake or Gordon?"

"Both," I admitted. "I've wanted to move here since I was at least sixteen years old. Did you know that?"

I already knew the answer, but I wanted to see him own it. "Of course I did. You had a poster of the Golden Gate Bridge on your wall."

"I told Gordon moving here was my dream on the very first night we went out. Do you know what he told me?"

"No. What?"

"He told me I'd like New Orleans better."

Scott was silent for a moment while that sank in. Then I continued.

"After we'd been dating seriously for a year, I told him my plan was to move to San Francisco after graduation. I wanted to find out what he had in mind so we could plan together. That's when he told me he was joining the air force. He never even asked my opinion—just told me like it was a done deal. So we broke up when he went in. If we stayed together and he served in the Armed Forces, I'd never get a chance to move to the States."

"But that's when Nana went into the home," Scott murmured to himself.

"Yes. So, instead of moving here, I stayed and started nursing school in Edmonton so I could be with her," I admitted. "And I never regretted those two extra years we got with her, Scott."

"She loved you, Noah. You were always her favorite. I never understood your desire to be a nurse until I saw you with her those last couple of years. You're really good at it."

Hearing those words from my brother made my eyes sting and my shoulders relax.

"Thank you."

Scott thought for a minute. "So even if things were fine with you and Gord, you'd never be able to follow your dream."

He finally got it. I met his eyes. "And fine isn't good enough for me anymore, Scott. I deserve more than fine."

"You're right. Of course you do. So where are you going to go?"

I looked at him for a moment while I debated what to tell him.

"I'm going to find Luke."

He knew exactly what I meant because he could barely refrain from rolling his eyes. "Shit, Noah. Not this again."

I felt my hackles rise, but I didn't say anything.

"Isn't Luke dating an underwear model?"

Now my hackles had hackles. "No. He was sleeping with one, not dating him."

"What's the difference?"

I couldn't help but sigh in frustration. "Look, nothing good is going to come of this conversation, so why don't we just stop right here."

Scott gripped my upper arm gently. "Noah, I worry about you. We all do. As much as I'd love to have you stay home with Luke where you're safe, you and I both know he's not the long-term-commitment type."

Despite my best efforts not to be a whiny brat, I stuck my chin up in the air. "So?"

"So... he's just going to fuck you and leave you, Noah. And then your heart's going to be broken. You've had a crush on him since we were kids. The person you think he is isn't the one he actually grew up to be."

"How the hell do you know? You haven't lived in the same town with Luke in over fifteen years. I live with him."

"He's a playboy," Scott said gently.

"He's sweet and thoughtful."

"Maybe, but he's never been in a serious relationship, brother."

I couldn't argue the facts, but how could I tell him I knew in my gut Luke and I belonged together? Even though I recognized I was flip-flopping over Luke, I still knew I couldn't just let it go without a fight.

"There's a first time for everything, Scott," I said instead. "I have to go."

"Don't do this, Noah. You're going to get hurt," he warned.

I gave him a quick hug and stole my coffee from the tray on the table. It wasn't until I was out on the sidewalk in the cold winter air that I responded under my breath.

"Too late."

BY THE TIME I'd gotten up the nerve to call Jasmine and demand Luke's location, I'd gone from determined to disgusted with myself.

Scott was right. Of course he was. Luke wouldn't want me. I was turning out to be the sniveling brat he always remembered me as. But it's not like Luke hadn't known that about me, and I'd told him, begged him, not to start something with me if he was just going to pull back again.

Hadn't I?

Yes. I had.

Motherfucker. Okay, now I was angry. Madder than hell, and I wanted revenge.

Jasmine's voice was concerned as soon as she answered the phone. "Noah?"

"How'd you know it was me?" I asked, ducking under the awning of a hotel nearby to get out of the foot traffic on the pavement.

"Luke made me program your number into my phone so I'd be sure to answer if you ever needed anything. Are you okay?"

That fucker. That sweet, thoughtful *asshole*.

"No. I need to see him. Where is he, Jasmine?"

There was a pause so I pushed forward. "Don't even think about not telling me, dammit," I growled.

"He's my boss, Noah."

"Yeah, and he's a motherfucker. I need to see him right fucking now."

She laughed. "Oh, sweetie. I knew when he finally got real feelings for someone, the man would be a keeper."

"He'd be lucky to keep me, Jasmine, but at this rate, you and I are the only ones who feel that way. He's a goddamned coward."

"Noah, go easy on him. He clearly doesn't know what the hell he's doing. He's never truly fallen for someone before. At least, not since I've known him."

That stopped me in my tracks.

Fallen for someone? As in, falling in love?

With me?

I exhaled a white vapor cloud into the cold, damp air. "Where is he, Jazz?"

"The vineyard. But you didn't hear it from me."

It took me over twenty-four hours to find my way there, but when I finally arrived, I still hadn't figured out whether I was there to tell him off or beg him to take me.

18

THE MARIANS - SATURDAY TREE-TRIMMING AT THE VINEYARD

Every year the tree seemed to get bigger. Not that the girls cared. Pete and Ginger's twins were the only ones old enough to scale the tall ladder besides the adults, so they took great pride in making sure the tree was adequately enormous and challenging to decorate.

"Pass me that eggnog, Tristan," Granny said from her spot in the corner of a giant L-shaped sectional sofa.

"It's baby formula, Granny," Blue replied. "If you want eggnog, I'll have to go back to the house."

"Why's it in a pitcher?"

Tristan picked up the pitcher and began filling baby bottles on the portable bar that had been set up in the corner of the room. "Because I'm making enough for Wolfe, Benji, and Mattie."

Tilly piped up from her spot at a table where she worked on a puzzle. "He said the name, you all have to drink."

Three or four Marians obediently took sips of their drinks without even asking what the hell she meant. Blue looked at Tristan with furrowed eyebrows. "What was that about?"

Granny rolled her eyes. "Tilly's ego is out of control ever since you two named that girl after her. Couldn't you have named her after me instead?"

Blue laughed. "I'm not sure even Tristan knows your real name, Granny."

"Bullshit," she spat. "Everyone knows my name is—"

She was interrupted by a loud wail from the baby in question. Irene, who was holding Mattie, held her out from her body as if she'd detonated a bomb.

Dante was the first to jump up and offer to take her. "Come here, gorgeous girl. Uncle Dante will take you for a diaper change."

AJ's eyes tracked Dante's progress across the open lobby area to the guest rooms beyond before he must have decided he didn't want to miss out on the opportunity to get Dante relatively alone for a few minutes. He scurried along behind him.

Tristan leaned in and landed a soft kiss on Blue's temple. "Remind me to leave this vineyard to your baby brother in my will," he murmured.

"No kidding," Blue said with a laugh. "If only we could get him to relocate the Marian House shelter to Napa, we'd have the best babysitter ever."

Their toddler, Ella, played quietly on the thick rug in front of the fireplace. She was the quieter of their two girls and prone to being fawned over by all the members of the extended Marian clan. Mattie, on the other hand... Well, Mattie wasn't quite so docile.

Jude and Derek came through the glass double doors into the lobby.

"Sorry we're late," Derek called out. He held eight-month-old Wolfe in one arm and Jude's hand in the other. Wolfe's dark hair stuck out everywhere and his face was flushed pink. He had the glazed look of a baby who'd just woken up from a nap.

Simone stood up to grab her nephew, but Pete and Ginger's daughter Chloe beat her to it, grabbing him from Derek's arms to take him to the bar where Hazel helped Tristan close up all the bottles.

"Where are your bags?" she asked. "Aren't you staying the weekend like the rest of us?"

"Yes, they're in the car. We're staying with Tristan and Blue at the house, so we'll get them later," Jude said. "Where's Mom?"

Pete answered from up on the ladder where he and Sam were finishing stringing the lights on the tree. "They're taking a walk around the lake."

Griff had been dozing in a chair with four-month-old Benji asleep on his chest, so he just lifted a hand in greeting rather than make a sound and risk waking the baby.

The only Marians unable to make it to the annual tree-trimming were Maverick, Beau, Thad, and his fiancée, Sarah. Mav and Beau lived in South Carolina and would be coming back in time to spend Christmas and New Year's at the vineyard. Sarah was working at the hospital on a case over the weekend, and Thad was overseas assisting an old colleague with a health-care initiative in South Africa. The plan was for everyone to be together there for Christmas itself, and Rebecca and Thomas were beside themselves with excitement getting ready for it.

In the meantime, the usual local Marians gathered to trim the tree and have a nice dinner together, and most of them would stay and hang out the following day as well.

Jude walked over to Jamie and reached out a hand to pet Sister where she lay on top of Jamie's feet. "Where's Teddy?"

He tilted his head toward the glass doors along the back of the lobby that led out to the lawn and the lake. "He snuck out to get some photos of Mom and Dad by the lake while they're not looking. I think he wants to frame one for them for Christmas and make copies for the grandkids."

Jude's smile brightened at the thought, and Jamie noticed Derek's face brighten as a result of seeing his husband happy. "That's thoughtful, Jame. Teddy always acts like a bumbling oaf, but he's really a sweetheart, isn't he?"

Jamie's face softened. "Yeah. Just don't tell him that. He has a reputation to uphold. His friend Mac warned me never to let his ego get too big."

"Or what?" Derek asked, sitting down next to his husband and pulling Jude onto his lap.

Jamie just looked at Derek with a raised eyebrow until all three of them began laughing. Clearly they all knew Teddy's head was already way too big, and there was nothing any of them could do about it.

A loud squawk turned everyone's head toward the guest room hallway where Dante and AJ emerged with baby Mattie. She didn't look any happier with a clean diaper than she had before, so one of the girls quickly shuttled a bottle over to her, handing it to Dante.

Once he began feeding her, a quasi-silence fell again as Chloe and Hazel sat down to do the same with Wolfe and Benji. It didn't take long before Ella realized she was the only Marian grandbaby without someone to snuggle her, and she determinedly made her way toward Great-Aunt Tilly's lap and climbed up.

Tristan gently elbowed Blue to get his attention, and the two fathers watched as their daughter asserted herself to take what she wanted.

What she wanted was Tilly.

Upward of sixteen Marians sat or stood around watching the sweetest, quietest Marian select the craziest one as her person.

It wasn't anything new. Ella had seen something special in Tilly early on and would get particularly calm and quiet when held in Tilly's arms. It wasn't until Ella was mobile and able to choose for herself that she began gravitating to Tilly whenever possible.

Tilly ignored everyone's eyes on her and narrowed her eyes at the little girl. "You feeling left out?"

Ella's huge dark blue eyes looked up at Tilly's faded ones.

"Well, come here, then," Tilly sighed, pulling Ella into her body and guiding the baby's sweet face onto her chest. "Let me tell you a story about your papa when he was a little boy."

Ella's chubby hand came out to play with the reading glasses hanging from a chain around Aunt Tilly's neck while Tilly spun a tale about Blue learning the "Twelve Days of Christmas" song backward one year during a big extended family Christmas dinner.

"You see, Uncle Peter was a mean older brother," Tilly continued in a deceptively sweet voice. Ginger snorted and looked at Pete, who just shrugged. "He taught it to Papa that way on purpose to confuse him. But what did your Papa do? Sang it as loudly and proudly as he could to anyone who would listen. Everyone thought it was adorable and fawned all over little Papa. Meanwhile Uncle Peter learned a valuable lesson."

Tristan piped up from where he'd sat on a sofa next to Blue. "That nothing is cuter than Blue Marian?"

Tilly shot him a look. "No."

Jude grinned. "That as long as you're confident in the performance, no one will notice your mistakes?"

Tilly shook her head again while making silly faces at Ella.

Simone scoffed. "That Blue has always been everyone's favorite?"

Tilly ignored her and glanced at Pete. "Peter?"

Pete climbed down from the ladder and plugged in the tree lights to massive applause.

"That your family will always love you, no matter what."

Granny rolled her eyes and reached for a nearby liquor bottle. "Christ on a cracker, since when did you become a sappy old lady? Mattie, Mattie, Mattie," she repeated, filling up three shot glasses and handing them all to Tilly. "There, now let's get this show on the road."

ONCE THE TREE WAS DECORATED, Chloe and Hazel helped hang all the stockings. Rebecca tried to hold back tears when she presented this year's new babies with their very own stockings. Wolfe's was in the shape of a guitar, Benji's was needlepointed with a roly-poly dragon on it that matched his dads' tattoos, and Mattie's had a black-and-white border collie on it that looked just like their dog, Piper. For some reason, Piper went everywhere Mattie went, despite the baby's terrible habit of screeching.

Rebecca took pictures of all the babies with their stockings before turning to Griff. "I got one for Pippa too. Do you know if Nico's coming home for Christmas?"

"I think they're staying in Texas, Mom. West wanted him to experience a Wilde Christmas. I would imagine it's pretty similar to ours. West has a ranch load of siblings," Griff said. "Plus, I'm not sure they wanted to travel with Pippa again so soon. After getting her through RSV, West and Doc are keeping a close eye on her this winter."

Thomas reached over and ran a hand through Rebecca's hair, pushing a thick lock behind her ear. "Why don't we fly out there and see them after New Year's? I know you miss them, Bec."

She smiled at her husband of forty years. "Yes. Let's do. I'd like that. I know he's happy there, but I don't like knowing he's so far away."

Tilly, Granny, and Irene had gone through the rest of the liquor bottle and requested another. Rather than give in to their demands, Tristan had convinced them to switch to Irish coffees.

So now they were drunk *and* caffeinated.

"The tree's crooked," Irene claimed, staring at the giant monstrosity by the fireplace. "Honey, get under there and tilt it."

Granny began the long, involved process of lowering herself to the floor while several Marian men yelped and jumped up.

"Granny!" Tristan cried. "No, I'll do that. Sit down."

Too late. Granny was already on the floor. She looked up at her grandson. "Might as well do it now that I'm down here."

Blue pushed Tristan closer to Granny. "Tris, so help me god, do not let your grandmother tilt the twenty-foot tree."

"She's stronger than she looks," Tristan muttered, reaching down to help her up.

Simone barked out a laugh. "No doubt. She's beaten me arm wrestling more times than I can count."

Granny waved Tristan off. "Leave me be. This rug is more comfortable than that damned chair. You need to send your man out to buy some better stuff for in here."

"Why me?" Blue asked.

"You're a designer," she snapped. "Plus, you're gay."

The room erupted in a mix of laughter and offended gasps.

Blue's was laughter. "News flash, old lady, so is Tristan."

Granny flapped her hand in the air. "Not really. He's just gay for you."

The volume in the room got even louder as the topic of conversation turned into a debate about whether that was even a thing.

Granny finally lost her shit. "Fine! So he's gay. He still can't decorate a room, and you all damned well know it. Stop pegging me as some kinda homophobe. I'm a goddamned lesbian, for pete's sake."

Irene walked up to lay a blanket over Granny. Her eyes twinkled down at her tiny wife. "And here I thought you were just gay for me."

Granny's face went soft as she met Irene's loving gaze. "Come down here, Reenie, and feel how soft this rug is."

"You're just trying to get me to snuggle you in front of the fire," Irene said with a smirk.

"Yeah. And?"

"And all you had to do was ask," she said, folding her long, willowy body down onto the rug beside Granny. The taller woman pulled Granny in close and wrapped her arms around her. "What's going on with you? There's nothing wrong with that chair you were sitting in," she murmured into Granny's ear.

"It didn't have you in it."

Quiet descended once again while the Marians gazed at Granny and Irene in front of the fire, Ella and her baby cousins all asleep in various portable cribs around the edges of the space, and the massive, beautiful Christmas tree sparkling with lights and family ornaments.

Suddenly, the double doors crashed open and an irate Noah Campbell came storming in.

"Where the hell is he?"

The Marians swiveled their heads around and gawked at him.

"Calm down," Dante pleaded, standing up and rushing to Noah's side. "Take a deep breath."

"I know Luke's here. Where is he?" Noah's eyes were wild and ringed in shadows as if he hadn't slept. "Took me over twenty-four damned hours to find this place."

Pete stood up from the sofa and walked over to where Noah stood in front of the reception desk. No one was manning the desk since the lodge was closed to visitors for the weekend.

"Have a seat, Noah," Pete said calmly. "Let me go see if he's up for a visitor."

"Screw that," Noah spat. "Tell him to get his ass out here whether he's up for it or not."

As Pete turned to walk down the guest room hallway, Noah seemed to realize what he'd walked in on.

"Oh god," he said in a whisper. "Oh god, I'm so sorry. I'm so, so sorry."

Dante threw an arm around his shoulders, and Ginger stood up to give him a hug.

"It's okay, Noah. You're always welcome here," Blue said with a smile. "Come have a seat."

But Noah was in no mood to sit still. He stormed down the guest room hallway after Pete.

19

LUKE

I'd slept for almost twenty-four hours straight. That is, if "slept" meant "tossed and turned and stressed without getting any actual sleep."

Finally, I must have somehow dozed because I came awake on Saturday late morning and had no clue where I was. It took me a minute to recognize the familiar guest room style of the Alexander Vineyard lodge. The four-poster bed and maple-hued furniture glowed warmly in the golden light sneaking around the curtain edges.

I stretched and sat up, remembering with a leaden heart what had led me there the day before.

Noah.

I wondered how things had gone Friday morning with Gordon. Had he made his bad behavior up to Noah? Had Scott pressured Noah to smooth things over with Gordon for the sake of the families?

I ran a hand through my hair in frustration. There was no way I was going to survive another full day of thinking about it and speculating. I was going to find a cup of coffee, catch up with Pete if he'd arrived yet with Ginger and the kids, and then go for a long run.

After I pulled on my running clothes and shoes, I made my way out to the lobby where I was lucky enough to find not only coffee, but a tray of complimentary Danish as well. The front desk clerk had just finished checking a young couple out when she approached me.

"I'm heading home for the weekend, so if there's anything else you need, just call Blue or Tristan, okay?"

I glanced at the empty front desk and then back at the woman. "You closing down or something?"

She smiled brightly. "Yep. Every year the Marians close the lodge on several occasions to have it all to themselves. This weekend is the tree trimming. Everyone should be here by lunchtime, and Sam will have food brought over from the restaurant."

"Oh, shit. Pete didn't mention it. Sorry," I said.

"It's no problem. You're listed in the system as family, Mr. Holland. Come join us anytime. There's always a room available for you," she told me before wandering off to gather her purse from behind the counter and exiting through the glass double doors to the small parking area out front.

I took my cup and plate over to one of the large sofas by the giant stone fireplace. The huge, empty Christmas tree had already been set up nearby and was clearly just waiting for attention from Pete and his family. Hearing that they considered me an honorary Marian made me feel warm and comforted, especially so far away from home.

My own family was made up of just my aunt and uncle now. I loved them for sure, and spent most Christmases back in Cold Lake with them. But it wasn't the same as having my own parents.

My dad had worked in the oil sands and died in a work site accident when I was only eight. After that, Mom had become a serial monogamist, dating one man after another in a bizarre effort to find a replacement for my dad before she'd finally succumbed to what my aunt still insisted was a broken heart. By the time Mom died when I was eighteen, I'd tried learning not to attach myself to the boyfriends she brought home. Everyone who came into our lives wound up leaving eventually. Either it wasn't love, or love never lasted.

Knowing I had the stable, loving Marian family here in the States was more of a comfort than I'd expected. While it was hard to wrap my head around so many committed relationships in their family, seeing the love between them all was a gift I was grateful for.

I gazed into the fireplace and couldn't help but think of Noah. I loved how the Marians had taken him in too. They'd recognized right away he needed them, and they'd welcomed him into the fold immediately.

"There you are," Pete said, wandering through the doors the receptionist had just exited. "Find something to eat?"

I held up my plate and coffee. "You didn't tell me it was a big family to-do this weekend."

He waved his hand. "Nonsense. You know Mom and Dad. The more, the merrier. Especially at the holidays. They're all coming in today to trim the tree this afternoon, and you're welcome to join us. But what's going on? Why'd you want to get away this weekend?"

I glanced away at the crackling fire in the fireplace. The logs were huge and thick to fit the giant opening.

"The Samari case. Just wanted to be able to focus without distractions," I lied.

Pete studied me. "If you say so, man. But you know you could also tell me the truth if you wanted. I won't bite."

I clacked my teeth together. "I'm fine. Just have a lot on my mind."

"And is one of those things a certain nurse who also happens to know his way around a set of vibrator attachments?"

I laughed unexpectedly. "Shut up. So what if it is? I just needed some space."

He patted my knee before standing back up. "Hey, if you want a running buddy, I'm sure Ginger would love to go with you."

He headed down the guest hallway toward what I assumed were his family's rooms, but he called out one last thing over his shoulder.

"And Luke? Just don't forget *space* can get awfully lonely."

BY THE TIME I saw Pete again, I'd taken that long run with Ginger and returned to my room to shower and make an effort to actually work on my law case. It was late afternoon when Pete knocked on my door.

"Someone's here to see you," he said tentatively when I opened the door.

"Who?"

"Noah. And he looks like he's been crying." Pete's expression was accusatory, which was unnecessary. My throat tightened.

"Where is he?"

Before the words were even out of my mouth, I saw him. Rather, I heard him.

"Move," he told Pete, nudging him out of the way and striding past me into my room. I almost laughed at the determination on his face, but I could tell that wouldn't be well received.

I looked back at Pete. "I'll take it from here."

"Don't hurt him," Pete warned me.

Noah scoffed from behind me, and Pete glared at him next.

"Don't hurt *him*, either," Pete said to Noah.

Noah's eyes widened, but before he opened his mouth to respond, Pete was gone. I closed the door gently and turned to look at him.

He looked like shit.

And he was the most beautiful thing I'd ever seen.

How was that possible?

"Hi," I said stupidly.

"I hate you."

The lump in my throat got bigger, and guilt threatened to overwhelm me. I hated seeing him so upset. I should have never come on to him. I should have protected his heart by staying well away from him. I was such a fucking idiot.

"I understand," I said calmly.

"You promised," he accused. I could hear the tears threatening. "I told you not to toy with me, and you promised."

"No, I didn't." I specifically remembered kissing him instead of saying the words since I hadn't been able to keep my hands off him long enough to promise.

"You did, Luke. You *did*." The tears brimmed in his eyes now, threatening to spill over, and I couldn't take it.

"Noah," I said, moving toward him.

"No," he sobbed. It was a plea. Another beg, but this time it was to stay away rather than come close. He held his hand out as if that would stop me.

"I'm sorry," I began.

"I don't believe you."

"You're angry."

He let out a cross between a laugh and sob. "You don't even know angry."

I needed him to let me touch him, to let me comfort him.

"Please come here," I said in a whisper. "Even if you hate me and even if you're angry at me. Please let me hold you for just a minute. Please, baby."

His eyes bore the pain of a thousand cuts. "You don't get to call me that."

"Okay. I won't even talk. Just let me hold you until you're not so upset anymore."

As I spoke, I moved closer and closer until I was able to wrap my arms around him and pull him in tight.

He surrendered.

All of the anger and hurt and confusion came out of him in waves as he sobbed into my chest.

There were so many things I wanted to tell him. About why I was terrified of letting anyone get close to me—about the fact I'd always been told attorneys made shitty spouses. About how hard it was for me to trust that he would want to stick around longer than a few months when no one else ever had. But I'd promised him I wouldn't speak, and I was damned sure going to honor my promise to him now.

My lips rested in his hair and my arms held him tightly until I felt him wind down. I led him over to my bed and pulled back the covers.

"I'm not sleeping with you," he said defiantly.

"I just want you to rest. I can leave if you want."

Noah looked at me for a minute before giving in. "Fine. You can stay. But I'm keeping on the sweats."

I refrained from pointing out they were my sweats. Had he been wearing them for almost two days since I'd seen him put them on?

After nudging him over in the bed, I slid in behind him. The bulky hoodie he wore was going to block my access to him, so I got back up to grab a clean T-shirt out of my bag.

"Here, at least swap out the hoodie for this," I said softly.

He did as I said, exposing the wide strong back I'd spent hours mapping with my tongue only a few nights before. I had to force myself to look away if I had any hope of lying in that bed with him without making a move.

Once he was settled again, I spooned in behind him and let out a breath against his neck.

This.

This was exactly where I was supposed to be.

I drifted off immediately into a deep, dreamless sleep.

But when I awoke, Noah was gone. And this time, I had a feeling it was for good.

20

NOAH

You know what makes heartbreak even more of a motherfucker? When three little old ladies try to hook you up with the local motor-cycle club of leather daddies.

After I'd woken up in Luke's arms and forced myself to gather up my dignity and leave, Dante had offered for me to move in with him and AJ through the holidays. Honestly, I hadn't wanted to inconvenience them, but the thought of living with Luke right now was next to impossible. Clearly he hadn't wanted me the way I wanted him. I'd made the big gesture, navigated my ass all the way to Napa, and he'd just... what? Told me he'd never made me any promises?

Fuck, I was stupid and naive. Desperate and immature too.

Thank god for Dante's offer. There was no way I'd be able to keep my shit together if I had to see Luke every day. And what the hell would I do if he brought a man home to the apartment?

No.

No fucking way.

So I'd accepted and moved in to Dante and AJ's spare bedroom. It turned out to be lots of fun because AJ was working on some kind of rescue case that took him out of town on a business trip, which meant

Dante and I could keep each other company with video games and binge-watching holiday movies.

It was wonderful, right up until Aunt Tilly showed up and lied to my face.

"Be a dear and accompany me to a fundraiser this afternoon, Noah," she said, breezing into Dante and AJ's apartment like she owned the place. A thick cloud of fancy perfume followed in her wake.

I glanced at Dante who just sighed in defeat. "Tilly," he warned halfheartedly.

"You," she snapped, pointing at him. "Zip it. I need Noah to come with me to Mary Edward Coppenheim's Cookie Exchange for Convicts."

"What for?" I asked. I'd been around her enough by that point to be suspicious.

"My friend Omi is planning a trip to Alberta next summer. I told her I'd bring you so you could give her all the best places to visit."

Lie. Total lie.

"Fine. But there'd better be actual cookies there," I muttered, wandering back toward my room to change into some nicer clothes. "And no convicts!" I called back to her over my shoulder.

It turned out that Mary Edward had a son named Humphrey. The man was fifty years old if he was a day, and because he was the creepy uncle who'd never been married, his mother had assumed he was gay. She'd taken it upon herself to matchmake the shit out of him.

I felt his pain.

Even so, it took all my self-control not to call him Humph.

I tried my best to be polite. "So... ah, Humph... rey... what do you do for work?" I shoved a pink cookie in my mouth to keep from saying anything further.

"Dance," he said in a monotone. I was busy trying to ignore the smear of something vaguely cream-colored on the thick lens of his eyeglasses. Frosting, maybe? *Please, god, say it was frosting.*

It took a moment for his single word to filter through my distraction. I tilted my head at him. "I'm sorry, did you say you *danced* for a living?"

I heard Tilly choke on something, but I didn't even turn to make sure she was okay. She could suffocate for all I cared.

"Square," he said, coughing up some phlegm. "I teach square dancing."

I blinked at him.

He continued. "I could take you some time. Give you a free lesson. You like banjo music?"

He pulled a well-used brownish handkerchief out of his pocket and blew his nose.

"I feel like there's some banjo music playing here right now. Yes?" I asked vaguely, looking around.

"Naw, that's just Jimbo," he said with a snort. As if that was all the explanation I needed. I didn't dare ask what a Jimbo was.

"Where's the restroom?" I asked as politely as I could.

"Come on, I'll show you," he said with a creepy grin. "You can check out my room. I have crabs."

Oh dear god.

I shot a look at Tilly that promised a long and tortuous revenge. She narrowed her eyes at me, reminding me who would always have the upper hand between the two of us.

It was her.

Luckily, Humphrey's crabs were of the hermit variety, much like himself, and I enjoyed seeing the delight the little dudes gave him. I came to understand that his lack of dating life was probably more about his mother's tight control over him than anything else. He wound up confiding in me that he'd had a crush on his mother's friend Doris for twenty years. The way he talked about her, I began to wonder if there wasn't some actual Mrs. Robinson nookie shit happening behind the scenes.

No matter. None of my business.

Once we were safely back in Tilly's town car, I turned on her.

"Never again. Promise me."

"I will not. That poor boy needed a friend."

"Tilly, he has fifteen hermit crab besties, and the last thing I need is Mary Edward breathing down my neck wondering when I'm going to give her grandbabies."

I couldn't say it without laughing, and before long, Tilly and I had tears streaming down our faces.

"Besides," I said. "He's banging someone named Doris."

"Crap, I knew it!"

"It's been going on for years," I told her.

"That skanky ho," Tilly said with what sounded like admiration. "Who knew she had it in her? Score one for retired librarians everywhere."

We laughed the rest of the way back to Dante's apartment where she let me out. After kissing her cheek, I stepped out and met her eyes through the open car door. "No more. And don't let Granny and Irene try either."

"Oh, no. They've got the perfect man for you. Had to tap a bunch of asses to find just the right guy."

I stared at her.

"Wait. I don't have the lingo right. On the screen. You have to tap them to get to their profile, right?"

"Are you talking about Grindr? For real?"

"Yeah, that. But don't worry. They found one for you. A grinder," she assured me. "You're a bottom right? A power bottom or..."

I slammed the car door and walked away.

As MUCH AS the meddling was annoying, it was also kind of comforting. The Marians were gathering around me like a warm, familiar jacket, and I knew they cared about my happiness.

After the dramatic scene at the vineyard, I'd tried to apologize for barging in, but none of them would have it. They'd asked what was going on between Luke and me, and I'd waved it off.

"Roommate shit," I'd said. "My brother and ex-boyfriend showed up out of the blue, and I overreacted. Luke felt kicked out of his own apartment, and I wanted to make sure he knew it was safe to come home."

Surely they'd all known that could have been accomplished with a simple phone call instead of a twenty-four-hour epic saga of trying to rent a damned car in a strange city and find my way out to a vine-yard in the middle of nowhere. But, thankfully, no one said anything.

And after that weekend, they were even more determined than ever to set me up on dates. I didn't have the nerve to ask if it was because Luke had said something—something putting a stop to any rumor that there was anything between the two of us.

Which, of course, there wasn't. Never would be. I could see that now. For whatever reason, relationships weren't his thing.

But they were mine. And having his arms around me, holding me, comforting me, was enough to remind me that I loved being with someone. I wanted that again. It had been almost a year since things had been good like that with Gordon. And even then, they hadn't been anywhere near as good as that. Being with Luke had woken me up to the fact I could find better than Gordon Ewing. Much better.

Therefore, I was determined to be open to finding it.

My next date was with Jude's friend Baker. He was an assistant music producer and had invited me to attend a holiday concert Jude and The Saints were putting on at the Fillmore. I was beyond excited to see Jude's band play, especially since they didn't tour anymore.

The band's live shows were currently limited to a few big ones around the country per year along with several more local ones where Jude could go perform and still kiss Wolfe good night when he got home. The band hadn't ruled out touring in the future, but Dante had told me he'd be surprised if they didn't take off at least one or two full years while Wolfe was still a baby.

Tonight's show was exciting because the San Francisco Gay Men's Chorus was being featured on stage for part of the performance. I had read about their Lavender Pen tour and couldn't wait to hear them sing.

When Baker picked me up at Dante and AJ's apartment, I'd finally morphed from excited for the concert to nervous as hell about meeting Baker. Fortunately, the man on the other side of the door was adorable.

"Hi," I said. "Baker?"

He was about my height, a couple of inches under six feet, and had wavy blond hair and friendly blue eyes. He was dressed in dark slacks and a red crew-neck sweater with a reindeer on it whose antlers were tangled in Christmas lights.

"Ahh," I said, trying to keep from laughing. "Nice sweater. Maybe I should change into something more... festive?"

Baker's cheeks turned pink as he realized what he was wearing. "Oh god. Shit. I'm so sorry." He looked up at me in horror. "My parents made me go to a thing, and I... fuck."

I finally let out a chuckle. "It's okay. It's kinda cute."

His rueful grin was charming. "Would you mind swinging by my place so I can switch it out really quickly? I don't live very far from the Fillmore. You can stay in the lobby while I run up if it'll make you more comfortable. I swear it's not a ploy to—"

I cut him off with a hand on his arm. "It's fine. We have plenty of time."

When we got to his apartment, I came up for a glass of wine. Baker went back to his room to exchange the red sweater for a dark luxurious cashmere number that begged to be touched. Too bad my hands were happier tucked into my own pockets.

But the conversation was easy and the man was sweet as hell. We wound up enjoying ourselves so much, instead of going to dinner at a restaurant, Baker pulled out some fancy meats and cheeses with crackers. While he busied himself setting them on a platter with some grapes, he peered up at me.

"I probably shouldn't admit this, but I was supposed to bring these to my parents' holiday thing and forgot. I'm not normally such an airhead, I promise." He slid the platter across the kitchen island and walked around to take the stool next to mine. "I was just preoccupied with anticipating our date tonight, to be honest."

"Really?" I asked. "Curious what real-life Canadians are like?"

He laughed softly. "Maybe. But Jude told me how genuine you

were and how sweet. Coming from someone as soft spoken as Jude, that's quite a compliment."

"He's definitely nothing like the person he portrays to his fans, is he?" I reached for a bite of cheese and stacked it with a fancy slice of salami on a cracker before taking a bite.

"Nah. Super hard worker and the kinda guy who would give you the shirt off his back." Baker took a few bites of the food also before continuing. "You ever heard them play?"

I shook my head. "Not live, no. Believe it or not, the only concert I've ever been to was Taylor Swift several years ago. She came to Edmonton, which is only a few hours away from my hometown."

"No kidding? God, Noah, we need to catch you up. I can get you in to see all kinds of great bands. San Francisco has amazing shows."

We continued eating, drinking, and chatting until it was time to go to the concert venue. Jude had made sure we had incredible seats right up front, and I probably spent the entire couple of hours with my head back, eyes bugged out, and mouth open in awe.

They were amazing.

At one point during a slow song called "Invisible," Baker reached over and took my hand. The gesture was sweet and appropriate but felt so wrong; I thought my stomach was going to turn inside out. I didn't want to hurt his feelings so I left my hand in his.

But it didn't feel right. And I felt like I was cheating on Luke, which only made me feel even stupider. When the song got to a line about green eyes sparkling, I felt Baker turn to look at me, but I couldn't bring myself to meet his eye.

What was wrong with me? Nice guy, wonderful evening, easy conversation and a gentle touch... Maybe I was broken.

My crush on Luke Holland had finally broken me.

When the show was over, Baker pulled me through the crowd and somehow got us access to a stage door. He led me through a maze of hallways he seemed to know by heart until we ended up at Jude's dressing room.

Baker nodded at the bodyguard and the man opened the door and called inside. "Derek, Baker's here."

We heard his muffled response to let us in.

I expected to walk into the room and pinch myself, but someone else was doing all the pinching. Jude had stripped off his black leather pants and stood there in a sweaty designer T-shirt and nothing but red-and-green-striped boxer briefs. Derek couldn't keep his hands off Jude's ass.

"Shit, sorry," I blurted, turning around to leave. Baker grabbed my arm to stop me.

"Don't bother. They're like this all the time after a show. I'd say it's disgusting, but it's kinda hot."

He was right. But it was also sweet, because even though he was busy pawing at his husband, Derek was also encouraging him to drink a cold bottle of water and murmuring what a good job he'd done.

"I told you the crowd would go nuts for that Bob Seger number," Derek said, nuzzling his nose into Jude's damp hair.

"Gross, I'm sweaty," Jude said with a laugh. "Let me shower real quick."

"Bluebell, if you think your sweat turns me off, I've been sending you the wrong messages," he growled. The two of them disappeared into the small bathroom, and I felt myself stare after them.

"I want what they have," Baker said with a soft sigh. I turned to look at him and saw him gazing after them the same way I had been.

"Yeah," I agreed. "It's pretty incredible. All the Marians seem to have it. What's with that?"

I'd meant it as a joke, but the truth of it was plain for both of us to hear.

"Hell if I know," he said wistfully. "But I'm going to keep taking out sweet men like you until I find it."

After a few moments, his gaze turned to me, and I saw the intention in it. He was going to touch me, and I didn't want him to. Before he had a chance to step toward me, the dressing room door slammed open and an Amazonian woman bustled in.

"Goddammit, where is that skinny little fucker?" the woman snapped. She had hot pink hair and a cropped jean jacket over a black tunic and zebra-striped leggings. She also wore Doc Marten boots that looked like they'd been around the block a time or twelve. She glanced at me before nodding her head at the bathroom door. "They in there?"

I nodded.

"Fucking?" she asked.

I shrugged and tried to keep my eyeballs in my head.

"You speak?" she asked me.

I shook my head just to be on the safe side. She studied me for a minute before her face softened. "You must be Noah."

"Yes, ma'am," I said.

"I'm Ollie, Jude's ex-best friend."

"Hey, Ollie," Baker piped up from behind her. She turned around to assess him.

"Baker."

I didn't give him a chance to say anything further because I wanted to know more about this interesting woman. "Why *ex*-best friend?"

She focused back on me. "Because we brought Kevin's nieces to the concert, and made Jude promise he'd sing—"

"Forget it, Olls. No Rudolph. The band vetoed it. Take it up with them," Jude said, coming out of the bathroom with a small towel over his wet head. His and Derek's matching flushed faces answered Ollie's earlier question anyway. Lucky bastards.

I tried not to think of Luke sucking me off in a shower.

I failed.

21

LUKE

The following week was awful. After waking up Saturday evening to an empty bed, I'd wandered out of my room to find several of the Marians finishing dessert around the lit Christmas tree. Blue had seen me first.

"Noah left," he'd said with sympathy all over his face. I hadn't been able to stand the idea of any of them seeing how bothered I was by the situation so I'd shrugged.

"His brother is in town. It's good he left so they can spend time together. I'm sure Scott's missed him," I'd said.

I could have sworn I'd heard Granny cough the word *bullshit* into her fist from her spot at the game table.

"What are you going to do?" Ginger had asked. She'd been holding one of the babies and from the wild dark hair, I'd guessed it was Jude and Derek's son.

"Nothing, what do you mean?"

"Give it up, Lucas," Ginger had sighed. "You're crazy about the kid."

"No," I'd lied. "Not true."

I'd sat down on the sofa next to Ginger and sighed heavily

without thinking. AJ had come over and sat on the heavy coffee table in front of me so he could face me.

"He's moving in with us," he'd said gently.

I'd felt the blood drain from my face. "Really?"

AJ's hand had come out to squeeze my knee. "Dante rode back to the city with him to help him move his stuff before you get home."

"Fuck," I'd muttered, sinking back into the deep cushions. "Dammit, I fucked up."

"Ya think?" Tilly had barked. "That boy shoots flowers and chocolates out his eye holes whenever he talks about you. And, what, you think you're too good for him? Asshole."

"Aunt Tilly," Pete had warned. "Give him a break. He's never cared about anyone like this before. The idiot doesn't know what he's doing."

He wasn't wrong.

I'd fucked up because I didn't know the first thing about having an actual relationship. I'd never trusted them. Every time my mom had claimed to love someone new, the relationship had crashed and burned within months. Was that what love was? Something temporary and fleeting? If so, I didn't want anything to do with it.

A part of me wondered if love was what my parents had experienced together. But if that was the case, having it and losing it had ruined my mother's life. How in the hell could I want that? Moreover, how could I let that happen to Noah? What if I tried to love him and wound up hurting him because I didn't know what the fuck I was doing?

I'd left there the following day determined to ignore the entire thing. I was way too busy and important to need to worry about a bunch of relationship bullshit. This entire scenario was proof of why I didn't do relationships. They were full of drama. All drama and no reward.

Of course a sneaky voice in my head reminded me of all the things about Noah that would be considered reward. But hell, I could have those without strings anyway, right? All I had to do was call

Victor, and I could have a hot mouth on my cock whenever I wanted it.

And if I wanted someone to stay the night and pretzel his legs with mine, I had a contacts list full of guys who'd wanted to stay and cuddle when I'd kicked them out after sex in the past.

But, of course, I was full of shit. Absolutely full of cocky nonsense. I didn't want Victor's mouth. I wanted Noah's. I didn't want to cuddle with just anyone. I wanted to wrap my arms around Noah and keep him safe through the night—my nose buried in his neck inhaling the warm sleepy scent of him.

And so it went. My brain ran laps around itself all week until I finally realized I had two choices: I could let him go and try to move on once and for all, or I could fight like hell to convince him this time was different and I was really in it with him.

Which meant there was really only one choice.

I had to get him back.

∾

IT STARTED WITH A TEXT EXCHANGE.

Luke: *Hey. Can I call you? I'd like to get together and talk.*

Noah: *I don't think that's a good idea.*

Luke: *Please, Noah. I want to apologize. To explain.*

Noah: *You already did.*

Luke: *I'd like you to come back home.*

Noah: *LOL you sound like Gord. No thanks.*

Luke: *Can I please take you out on a date again? Can we start over?*

Noah: *No. I don't want to do one step forward and two steps back anymore with you. Just leave it, Luke.*

Luke: *What do I have to do to convince you it will be different this time?*

Noah: *Time travel?*

Luke: *If I could, I would. I was an idiot.*

Noah: *Don't hold your breath waiting for an argument from me.*

Luke: *I'd like to tell you some things about me that might help you understand.*

Noah: *That's not necessary. I think it was my fault for not listening to you in the first place. You tried to tell me. I get it now. You're not looking for a relationship.*

Luke: *What if I changed my mind?*

Noah: *I should have never tried to be more than friends. I loved being friends with you.*

Luke: *Me too. I miss my friend Noah.*

I didn't hear back from him for a couple of days after that. I heard through the grapevine he was still going out on dates the Marians set him up on. I wanted to be mad at them for choosing sides, but I couldn't. I could only be thankful they tried to help him find happiness.

But I could admit it drove me up the fucking wall, especially when Jasmine admitted seeing Noah at a breakfast restaurant with Jude's friend Baker on Saturday morning.

"Not gonna lie, Luke. The kid was smiling from ear to ear," she said Tuesday morning in the office. "And I heard them talking about a concert of Jude's the night before. You don't think he spent the night with the guy, do you?"

I dropped my head into one hand and reached out to shoot her the bird with the other. She ignored me.

"Supposedly he has a date with Jamie's friend Josh sometime this week. You know, the park ranger from Denali? He's planning on taking Noah skiing in Tahoe overnight."

My stomach turned, and I wondered if I might need to vomit. I remembered Josh being the one Noah thought was particularly sweet.

"Stop," I begged her. "I can't take it."

"Well, if it makes you feel any better, apparently Granny and Irene took him to a leather bar Saturday night. He walked in, took one look around, and walked right out. Granny was pissed. She convinced Irene to stay with her at the club after sending Noah home in an Uber."

I looked up at her with quirked eyebrows. "Where are you getting all this information?"

She rolled her eyes. "Pete's paralegal, Neffi. She's the worst gossip in the entire office. Don't ever tell her anything you don't want everyone to know."

The rest of the morning was spent trying not to picture Noah spending the night in a cozy hotel room in Lake Tahoe curled up with a sexy park ranger.

I couldn't stand it. So I picked up the phone to text again after lunch.

Luke: *So, ah, I was thinking.*

Noah: *Don't hurt yourself.*

Luke: *There's a showing of To Catch a Thief tonight at that same theater we went to. Come with me? As friends.*

I didn't get an answer for fifteen long minutes.

Noah: *Just friends? Promise?*

Luke: *Yes, of course. Meet you there at seven?*

Noah: *Okay.*

I blew out a breath and must have cracked my face, grinning as I was from ear to ear. Even two hours later when I closed down my computer and walked past Jasmine's desk, it must have still been there.

"What the hell?" she muttered. "You smoking a bowl in there?"

"Nope. Just happy. See you tomorrow."

"What's going on?" she asked with suspicion.

"Noah agreed to go see a movie with me, that's all. Just friends."

Her expression softened. "Go slow, Luke. He's running scared. You gotta give him room to get used to the idea. Build up his trust again."

"I know," I assured her. "If he needs us to just be friends. I'm gonna friend the shit out of him."

I walked out with a spring in my step and the sound of her laughter in my ear.

～

"CARY GRANT, AM I RIGHT?" Noah sighed as we shouldered on our coats and left the theater.

Things had been awkward at first when we'd met in front of the theater, but as soon as we'd bought drinks and a tub of popcorn to share, I'd asked him if he'd seen the highlights of the Oilers game the night before, and he'd lit up. We'd stuck to sports and bullshit until the movie started, and by the time the movie was over, I'd felt like both of us had let go of the awkward tension and allowed ourselves to slip back into a comfortable friendship.

Apparently, the elephant in the room was dead asleep, which was fine by me.

"You hungry?" I asked once we hit the sidewalk. "I could go for something small. A salad or appetizer maybe."

He looked up at me and thought for a minute. "Yeah, okay. I could eat. Maybe that pub you mentioned a while ago?"

"Yep, perfect. It's this way just a few blocks," I said, resisting the urge to grab his hand as I turned to lead us in the right direction.

After we'd been walking for a minute, I asked him something I'd been wondering about. "Were you able to spend any time with Scott?"

"Yeah, actually. We talked before I left for... ah... Napa. And he finally seemed to understand why I left Gordon. I think while I was gone he and Gord talked about it. Or maybe Scott got Rose to talk to Gord. I don't know. But when I got back, the three of us were able to hang out a little bit, and it wasn't too weird."

"Good. I know the connection you and Gordon have though your siblings can't make the breakup easy."

"No, and if I was still living in Cold Lake, it might be harder. But I think it's going to be okay."

We walked in silence for a little bit before he took a breath. I could sense Noah looking at me out of my peripheral vision.

"I miss my friend Luke too," he said quietly.

I turned to look at him as he continued.

"You texted me that you missed your friend Noah. I just wanted you to know I missed you too. I'm sorry I fucked that up for us."

"It's not fucked up if we say it's not," I told him.

The smile he shot me was glorious.

"Yeah?"

"Yeah."

The rest of the evening was a kind of dance between us—a relearning of our boundaries. We obviously couldn't talk about dating or our love lives, and he got so flustered when I asked him about his Love Junk job, I decided to avoid it altogether.

But we had a million other things in common, and we found stuff to talk about all night. Finally, I realized we'd been at the pub for three hours.

"It's late," I said. "I have a client meeting at seven thirty tomorrow."

"Why so early?" he asked pulling out his wallet to split the bill. As much as I wanted to take care of it myself, I forced myself to let him pay his share the way a friend would.

"The guy has to fly out of the country, and it's the only time he could meet. We're hoping he's going to be back in time for a discovery hearing coming up. Trying to litigate this thing around his international travel has been a beast."

Once we'd paid and made our way outside, Noah turned to me.

"Thank you, Luke. I had a really nice time tonight."

His face began to turn pink in the cold night air, and his eyes were jade under the lights of the city street. I wanted to lean over and feel his warm lips on mine—take his hand and lead him home to my bed where he belonged.

"I had a nice time too. Good night, Noah," I said instead, before turning and walking away.

22

NOAH

After going to the movie with Luke, I went home to Dante and AJ's that night dizzy with a swirling vortex of emotions. Relief that things were okay between Luke and me. Disappointment they weren't better than okay. Desire for sexy times with Luke. Anger at him for being an immature playboy asshole who couldn't settle down with a good thing when it presented itself to him ass up.

But most of all, I felt a teeny-tiny shred of hope. The merest, slender sliver of possibility. I wasn't even sure what it was possibility *of*. Friendship? More? It didn't matter, really. I just knew Luke was back in my life in some form and I'd take it.

I fell asleep to dreams of a tall, dark and handsome man with a penchant for old Cary Grant movies. His hands were large and hungry, and his mouth was wet, swollen, and absolutely *everywhere* on my body.

When I woke up, I was already on the verge of coming. All it took was a few quick strokes of my fist around my throbbing cock before I bit his name into my pillow.

~

THE FOLLOWING EVENING, Simone Marian picked me up to take me out to dinner with her friend Joel Healy. Had it been anyone other than a Marian, I would have thought I was legit just going to meet a friend of hers for dinner. But this was a Marian.

So it was a date.

When I entered the restaurant, I saw a gorgeous tall bald man stacked with muscles. He wore black cargo pants with a black fleece pullover that had some kind of patches on it like he was in law enforcement or something. As soon as he saw us, his face lit up.

Correction: as soon as he saw *Simone*, his face lit up.

"Hey, beautiful," he said to her, leaning in to kiss her on the cheek.

I was dumbfounded for a moment. Was it possible Simone Marian, of all people, was just introducing me to a friend of hers and not really setting me up on a date?

I noticed her blushing. "Hi, Joel. This is my good friend Noah Campbell. Noah, Joel Healy. Joel owns On Your Six Security."

He shook my hand warmly and gave me a friendly smile. "Nice to meet you, Noah. She means I'm a meathead bodyguard."

"I didn't say that!" Simone argued. "Two of my brothers-in-law are meathead bodyguards, and I love them."

I'd never seen her flustered. It was kind of fun.

"You work with Derek and AJ, right?" I asked as we were led to a booth toward the back. Simone had picked a funky pizza place, and I was grateful to finally be able to relax somewhere without the pressure of it being a date.

"Well, Derek used to work with me, but now he only guards Jude's ass. AJ, on the other hand, works for me but not really as a bodyguard. He's a recovery specialist."

After Simone slid into the booth, Joel slid in next to her. I took the seat opposite. Simone looked uncomfortable so I shot her a look.

"Move," she said to Joel, nudging him with her elbow. "Over there." She gestured to my side with her head, and I stared at her. Joel looked confused.

"Ooookay. Sorry. Didn't meant to crowd you," Joel said to her before looking at me. "Do you mind some company?"

"Of course not," I said with a smile. It was one of those rare moments of making eye contact with another man and having a silent message of *Chicks, am I right?* pass between us.

"So, Joel," Simone began. "Noah is a nurse. He recently moved here from Canada and is going to be working in the emergency room."

Joel lifted a brow at me. "Really? That's great. Welcome to the Bay Area. You couldn't have connected with a better family." He turned back to Simone and gave her a megawatt smile.

She blushed but rolled her eyes and hid her face with the menu.

Once we'd ordered, Simone started again. It became clear to me fairly quickly she was trying to convince Joel I was the hottest thing since sliced bread. It was obvious she was trying to pair us up together. Which was ridiculous because even the toddler in the booth behind us could tell that Joel was into Simone.

She kept trying to hook me up with him, and he kept trying to hook her up with himself. Finally, I couldn't stand it any longer. I turned to Joel.

"Tell me about the last woman you dated," I said.

"Noah," Simone hissed. "What the hell?"

Joel glanced at Simone then me and back to Simone again. "You mean my late wife, Lena?"

I was pretty sure Simone's jaw had never dropped that low before. Joel's voice was hushed and reverent, and I could see Simone's heart growing at Mach speed in her chest like the Grinch's.

"You were married?" she asked softly. "I never knew that."

"It was a long time ago, Simone. I didn't want you to feel sorry for me or think I was still caught up on her memory."

The two of them locked eyes across the table, and I saw a very clear cue for me to go.

I nudged Joel in the side. "Sorry, I just remembered I told Aunt Tilly I'd deliver that Gingerbread Gyrator tonight. Gotta go."

Besides Joel letting me out of the booth, I'm not even sure they noticed me leave.

So after the botched date with Joel, the not-gay bodyguard, I was taken on a midweek overnight trip with Josh the adorable park ranger and our chaperones, Jamie and Teddy Marian.

Josh was as nice as could be, but he spent the entire trip gazing lovingly at Jamie. Teddy thought it was annoying as hell so he tried distracting himself with his camera. I thought Josh's obvious crush was a bit rude considering he was supposedly there with me, and Jamie was simply oblivious.

But the skiing was good, so there was that.

By the time Friday rolled around, I was ready for some down time. The Love Junk fundraiser at Harry Dick's was scheduled for Saturday night, and I knew I wouldn't be up for two late nights in a row. AJ had come home earlier that day, which meant he and Dante would most likely spend some significant alone time in their bedroom making up for lost time.

And I'd be odd man out.

I picked up the phone to text Luke.

Noah: *If Dante and AJ are going to have a fuck fest tonight, should I find somewhere else to be?*

Luke: *You don't want to be the Bird Wheel?*

Noah: *Ha ha. But no.*

Luke: *So come to my place— we'll get take out and watch a movie.*

Noah: *You don't have plans? It's Friday night.*

Luke: *I was going to take it easy because I'm going out to Harry Dick's tomorrow night to support a friend of mine who's doing a fundraiser.*

I caught myself smiling at that.

Noah: *You must really like that friend.*

Luke: *You have no idea. Come at eight?*

Noah: *I'll pick up Thai. The usual?*

Luke: *Apparently, I'm predictable.*

I picked up the two dishes we liked to split and made my way to the apartment. When he opened the door, Luke was barefoot in jeans and an old red Stanford T-shirt worn thin and soft from a million washings over the years. He looked good enough to eat.

I gulped.

"I carried a watermelon," I said lamely, quoting a movie and cradling the bag of food like a stack of firewood balanced on both forearms.

"Come in and get warm. Your face is red, you must have frozen out there." He grabbed the food from my arms so I could ease out of my coat and boots.

I didn't dare tell him the red face was from the dirty thoughts I was having about him.

"How was work?" I asked instead, following him to the kitchen to help pull out plates and utensils.

We chatted easily about our day while we sat down at his dining table to eat dinner. He'd already opened and poured a white wine he knew I liked, and I felt the comfort of his companionship and the familiar apartment surround me.

Once we were through eating, he refilled my wine glass and studied me. "I heard you skied Tahoe."

I snorted, remembering the disastrous dates I'd had this week. "I did. It was fun. Beautiful place. Have you been?"

"Yes, it's gorgeous. Why did you laugh though?"

I hesitated.

"Tell me," he urged with a smirk.

I sighed and smiled back. "I was set up. Again. Only this time it was with a guy who apparently still had the hots for Jamie Marian after three years of going out with the guy, like, once."

Luke laughed. "Oh god. You poor thing. How rude."

"No, that wasn't it. It was just... I don't know. I felt bad for the guy, you know? Pining after someone for so long when they clearly don't feel the same way..." I thought about what a waste of time it was to pine. It wasn't until I saw Luke's face that I realized he was making the connection between Josh and me. "No," I growled before I could help myself.

His eyes widened in surprise. "What?"

"Whatever you're thinking, stop. It's not the same."

"What was I thinking?" Luke truly looked perplexed. Maybe I'd misread it.

"Never mind," I muttered.

"Noah..." Luke began hesitantly.

I began to stand up to clear my dirty plate from the table. "Maybe this was a bad idea. I should go."

Luke's hand came out to lightly grasp my wrist, and I couldn't help but feel the heat from his touch all the way through my body.

"Stay. Please."

I exhaled and pulled away from him to continue gathering my place setting. "Fine, but let's watch the movie, okay? Enough talking."

He followed me into the kitchen with his own dirty dishes and told me to leave it all in the sink for later. After making our way into the living room, I sat down on one end of the deep sofa and he sat down on the other. Friends.

Sitting in the friend seats.

I tried not to chant a repetitive phrase in my head about this sucking.

This sucks. This sucks. *This fucking suuucks.*

Finally the movie began, and I let out another breath, trying hard to convince myself to chill the fuck out.

I must have taken the thought to heart, because before long, I chilled out so much, I fell dead asleep.

23

LUKE

He was out before the end of the first scene. I didn't realize at first until little snores started distracting me from the movie. Once I looked over and saw his relaxed face, I felt my heart swell.

He was curled up in a ball in the corner of the sofa with his head on the arm and his legs tucked up next to him on the cushion.

God, he was beautiful. His brown eyelashes skimmed the creamy skin of his cheeks and his lips were red and full. I hoped to god no other man had been allowed to kiss those lips since I'd been there last.

I clenched my fists in my lap to keep from touching him. My fingers itched to stroke inside the leg of his jeans to the muscled calf and beyond to where I knew hid the hem of a soft pair of colorful boxer briefs. I'd spotted them earlier as he'd leaned over to pick up a napkin he'd dropped on the floor. His shirt had ridden up, revealing a narrow sliver of the multicolor underwear. They had tiny Santa gnomes on them.

I was pretty sure my cock had been hard ever since.

For the next two hours, I alternated watching the movie and watching him. When the film finally ended, I moved over to brush a wayward strand of hair off his brow.

"Noah, you fell asleep. Do you want to just go to bed here in your old room?" I asked quietly. I moved my hand to cup his neck and ran my thumb along his jaw. "Baby?" I whispered.

He shifted and reached a hand out to rest on my inner thigh.

"Luke," he murmured. I was pretty sure he was still asleep.

I thought about leaving him asleep on the sofa, but I knew the following night was going to be a late one for him. He needed some good sleep.

After trying again and hearing him mumble for me to leave him on the sofa, I pulled him up over my shoulder in a fireman's carry.

That woke him up.

"Luke? What the hell?"

"Taking you to bed," I explained. Before he had a chance to sputter and argue with me, I added, "In your old room."

Once I set him down on the bed and pulled back the covers for him, he shucked off his jeans and shifted into bed. My jaw ticked from the effort it took not to stare at his adorable ass in those tight boxer briefs.

"You need anything?" I asked.

He blinked at me for a minute, still confused. "Luke?"

"Yeah?"

"Thank you."

Fuck. Me.

∾

THAT NIGHT at the club the Love Junk fundraiser went off without a hitch. Most of my friends were there, including many of the Marians. Noah's product presentations were hilarious. I could tell he'd gotten more comfortable with them since beginning his job because he only blushed when he looked in my direction. Even the five drag queens who'd volunteered as his spokesmodels didn't make him blush with all their fawning attention.

The club dancers were all over him—touching him, flirting with him, trying to pull him up on the platforms to dance with them. And the crowd loved it.

I did *not* love it.

After watching the scene play out for a couple of hours, I was on the verge of starting a barroom brawl when I felt an arm wrap around my waist from behind.

"Hey, stranger," a familiar voice drawled in my ear.

I turned to see Victor, all decked out in the latest club fashion with his hair styled just so and guy liner accenting his eyes.

"How've you been?" I asked over the loud music.

"Been missing your fine ass, if you want to know the truth. Dance with me."

I let him lead me out to the dance floor and put his hands on my hips as we began to move to the music. He was easy and free as usual, naturally garnering the attention of the men around us. He moved like liquid chocolate, decadent and sinful to the point you couldn't help but want a lick. I'd spent hours in the past enjoying Victor's body on the dance floor of clubs as a precursor to explosive sex. Sometimes we'd do it in the back of a club before even getting home to his place or mine. But tonight was different.

There was nothing in it for me at all. He was the same sexy man with the same sultry moves, but I still couldn't keep my eyes off the man with the bag of dicks by the stage.

I saw Noah glance at me and do a double take before his brows furrowed in recognition of my dance partner. He looked away and turned around to speak to one of the go-go boys who'd been flirting with him earlier.

Fuck.

I looked back at Victor. "I gotta go. Sorry, Vic."

He shrugged and turned around, no doubt looking for another man to grind against while I made my way over to Noah.

"Dance with me?" I asked from behind him in much the same way Victor had done to me earlier. The difference was I didn't touch him—only put my mouth next to his ear to speak the words so he could hear them above the roar of the club.

I felt his entire body shudder, but he shook his head no.

"Please, Noah. Dance with me," I said again. "Friends can dance together, can't they?"

Maybe it wasn't fair, throwing his words about being just friends back in his face, but it was all I could think of to get him to accept me.

I sensed him let out a breath before he turned around and nodded toward the dance floor.

Once we found a spot, I reached for his hip, but he backed up until he was out of my reach. The look on his face warned me there'd be no touching. Fine. I could live with that.

For now.

We danced like that for several songs—together but not touching —until a somewhat slower song came on. Noah turned as if to leave the dance floor for a drink, but I grabbed his hand and yanked him back toward me until he crashed into my chest. I tightened my arms around him to hold him close and leaned in to his ear.

"Please, Noah," was all I said.

I felt his body tense for another moment until he finally relaxed, tucking his face into my neck. If I wasn't mistaken, the tip of his tongue came out to take a swipe at the sweat there, as if to taste me. What I would have given to know what he was thinking in that moment.

We swayed to the slow sensual beat of the song as my hands rubbed around the expanse of Noah's back over his damp shirt. I felt Noah's hands curled up against my chest. I wanted to take him home where he belonged.

With me.

"Come home with me tonight," I murmured into his ear, taking the risk of nuzzling into him a little.

He shook his head and leaned back to look at me. His mouth tried smiling but his eyes carried a sad resignation that tore at my heart.

"I can't. I'm not built for short term, Luke. And you're not built for long term. Friends, remember? We're good at friends."

With my track record, how the hell could I argue with that?

A bartender I recognized from the club interrupted us to ask Noah for some help with the Love Junk merchandise, and Noah shot me an apologetic smile. He let the man lead him to where some men undoubtedly wanted to purchase something, and I was left to stare after him, wondering if that was truly the end of our potential for more than just friends.

I said my goodbyes to the friends I passed on my way to the door. I needed to leave before making a fool of myself with Noah again. If I put any more pressure on him for more than just friends, I'd lose him altogether.

Friends, Luke. Just cool the fuck down and give the man what he wants. He's not used to standing up for what he wants, but he's doing it with you. So honor that by being his friend.

I returned home to an empty apartment that screamed of Noah's absence. After downing a tall glass of water, I made my way to the guest room instead of my own bedroom. The sheets still smelled like Noah, so I stripped down and slid between them.

It was the only way I knew to lull myself to sleep.

24

NOAH

There were only five days left until Christmas. The fundraiser at the club had been a massive success, and I told Sally it would be my last sales event at Love Junk unless she needed me for a one-off event.

I'd heard from the head of the emergency room at the hospital that I could begin training the first week in January in anticipation of my license coming through a few weeks later. Knowing the life I'd planned in San Francisco was truly getting ready to begin was bittersweet.

I would be able to get my own place, but I'd miss living with Dante and AJ. Hell, if I was being completely honest, I really missed living with Luke most of all. Not because of the touching, even though that had been pretty stellar, but because of the easy companionship of living with someone else who enjoyed hanging out and watching hockey or going to an old movie, or checking out a new restaurant down the street on a whim. Luke had been the easiest person in the world to live with.

But I also knew that my shifts at the hospital would make it hard to date. As the new guy, I'd be more likely to work overnights and weekends until I built up seniority. Not that I minded. Sometimes I loved the alternately quiet peace and chaotic mess of the night shifts.

And weekend shifts went by so fast, they made my head spin. In a good way.

With that in mind, I planned to take advantage of a few more Marian setups.

Next on the list was a friend of Maverick and Beau's. I'd only met Mav and Beau very briefly at that first Love Junk party at the vineyard, but they'd arranged the date through Dante and encouraged me to meet the man named Hayworth.

Dante's smile as he described the guy was infectious. "He used to date Beau, but he was so deep in the closet, things didn't work out."

"Oh shit," I groaned. "Please tell me this isn't going to be like the date with Josh where he wouldn't stop fawning all over Jamie?"

"Nah, man. Hayworth is totally over Beau. He moved out west from South Carolina and has embraced the gay scene completely. Blasted out of the closet if you want to know the truth. Knows more clubs around here than I do."

I wasn't sure that was a good thing.

"What's he like?" I asked.

Dante was sitting sideways in a side chair by the TV with his legs over the arm of the chair. A small bowl of apple slices balanced on his stomach as he chomped away at one.

"Southern drawl to die for and courteous as the day is long. Cute. Real fucking cute. Let's see..." Dante thought for a minute before AJ wandered in from the kitchen with a soda.

"Didn't Luke go out with him once? You could ask him," AJ said, before taking a sip of his drink and plopping down on the floor with his back to Dante's chair.

Dante kicked his shoulder.

"Ow, what was that for?" AJ frowned.

Dante's eyes flicked at me and then back to his man. "Could you think before you speak, Angel?"

"It's fine," I said. "But it's not like I'm going to ask him about it."

I tried not to picture Luke and the faceless southern stranger going at it in Luke's bed. *Motherfucker.*

By the time Hayworth picked me up, I was wound up tighter than a shopper on Christmas Eve. They were right, though. He was cute and gentlemanly.

"I thought we could go ice skating down at the Embarcadero," he said with a friendly smile. "They're closed this evening for a private event. That's why I wanted to pick you up this afternoon. You sure that's okay? I know it seems a little odd starting a date this early."

I returned his smile and reminded myself to relax and have fun. I was going out with a handsome man in my favorite city during my favorite time of year. I was living the life I'd only ever dreamed about.

"Absolutely. Sounds awesome," I assured him.

As we made our way to that part of town, he walked me past the Macy's department store that featured huge display windows filled with rescue animals.

Hayworth placed his hands on my back to steer me toward them. "Do you mind if we stop and look for a minute?" he asked. "I missed it last year and really wanted to check it out."

The store windows were bright and colorful with a set decorated like a winter village. Nestled in and around the small buildings and trees were cat beds with real curled-up cats and kittens sleeping. Several others batted at toys that looked like snowflakes dangling from the ceiling.

"They do this every year?"

"Yeah. Cool, huh? They're all rescue animals up for adoption. I actually used to hate cats until my mom's cat had a litter of kittens when I was taking care of her. Gave me a different perspective." He let out a soft chuckle and I watched his face light up as he spied a fluffy white kitten pouncing on another one in the same area.

"What kind of cat is she?" I asked to keep up my end of the conversation.

"Persian—full-blooded with all the papers."

"Must have been some cute cotton ball babies then."

He shrugged. "They were mutts. All different colors. I'd accidentally let her out, not realizing she was in heat. But the kittens were the cutest fucking things ever. Wish you could have seen them."

"Whatever happened to them? Were you able to find homes for them, even though they weren't full-blooded Persian?"

"Yeah. In the end, people fought over them. A couple went to widowed friends of my great-aunt's. One went to my sister who fell in love with the little guy right away, and the last one is mine. He's at my apartment so maybe you could meet him some time." He turned to gaze at me with a smile on his face. It was nothing too forward, just enough to let me know he liked the idea of bringing me home to meet his cat.

I swallowed. "What's his name?"

"Beau," he said reverently.

I stared at him with my mouth open until he burst out laughing.

"I'm kidding, I swear. I just wanted to see the look on your face. His name is Chip—short for Chipmunk."

I felt my face heat. "Sorry for my reaction. It's just that—"

Hayworth reached for my hand to give it a squeeze. His smile was sweet and reassuring. "It's okay. Dante told me about your date with Jamie's friend. Thought I'd try and get a laugh out of you to put you at ease."

I laughed. "Oh my god. Talk about awkward. I'm not even sure it qualified as a date."

As we made our way to the outdoor ice rink, we continued holding hands as Hayworth chattered on about all of the things he loved about San Francisco. He seemed to have the same fascination with it I did, and I realized he'd be a good person to explore it with in the months to come.

Once we had our skates on, he looked over at me from his spot on the bench. "You know how to do this?"

"Please. I'm Canadian," I scoffed. "I was born on skates."

He looked back down at his rental skates. "Then, can you... ah... teach me?"

I tried not to laugh as I studied him. "You don't know how to skate?"

He threw up his hands. "Dude, I'm from Charleston, South Carolina. Why would I know how to ice skate?"

I held my hand out for him and he took it, carefully stepping his way across the rubber mats to the entrance of the rink. We started slowly—Hayworth's right hand on the side rail and left hand secured firmly in mine. After a few laps like that, he was ready to try it out on his own, and I let go and moved out to the middle.

I shouldn't have.

I heard some teenagers goofing around behind me and coming up quick. Before I could move back over to the side to get out of their way, someone rocketed into me, shoving me hard until my face met the ice and it felt like my skull cracked in half.

That was all I remembered of my date with Hayworth.

WHEN I FINALLY OPENED MY eyes expecting to see white ice in front of me, I saw white light instead. There were voices everywhere and beeping noises from machines.

"Am I dead?" I mumbled. "Is this the light we've all heard about?"

"He's awake!" I recognized the voice but couldn't place it.

"Back up and give him some space. Jesus." Another voice. Warm and loving, familiar. But again, I couldn't say whose it was exactly. It was like my brain and mouth couldn't quite work together to fit that last piece of the puzzle.

Different voices continued talking to me and about me.

"Noah, sweetie, how are you?"

"Goddammit, why'd you call us down here if he was still alive? I thought you said it was an emergency." That one was an old lady. One who I remembered had the ability to piss me the hell off at the drop of a hat.

"Granny?" I croaked. Wait, she wasn't my granny. Was she?

"I'm going to get something to drink," she said. "Call me when he codes."

I tried opening my eyes again but my head felt like it had been sheared in two. "Oh god," I whimpered, trying to bring my hand up to touch my head. A soft warm hand reached out for my wrist to stop me.

"Don't touch, sweetie. There's a bandage there." I was pretty sure it was Rebecca Marian. "You hit your head pretty badly."

The pain washed over me more fully as I became more alert and I felt tears leak out of my eyes.

"Luke?" I asked no one in particular. My voice sounded foreign, a pathetic whimper.

There was a beat of silence before several voices spoke at once.

Rebecca cut in with her soft but commanding tone. "Everyone, hush. His head is probably splitting. Noah, honey, we haven't been able to get a hold of him yet. Peter says he's in court, which means his phone is off. But we've all texted and left messages."

The room erupted into noises again—everyone reassuring me that he'd get the messages and come right away. I thought I heard Hayworth's voice, full of worry and guilt, but I didn't spare it a second thought. I'd tell him later it wasn't his fault. I wasn't sure exactly what had happened, but I knew it wasn't his fault.

Someone, Simone maybe, asked if I wanted them to contact my family. I grunted out a *no* and let myself slip back into unconsciousness.

25

LUKE

After waiting for our docket call since lunch, it was finally our turn at half past four in the afternoon. The hearing before ours had run way over, and I'd had to promise the judge ours would be short in order for him to agree to even hear it today.

The case was an intellectual property dispute between a software company and an independent consultant they'd hired to do some development work. The giant software company was suing the sole proprietor for theft of a piece of unrelated code he'd supposedly written while under contract to work solely for them.

Our client was the defendant, Hamid Samari, who claimed he'd never received a proper legal contract to cover said work product. In order for us to know what we were up against, we needed the company to present a copy of the contract they claimed he'd signed. Hence, the discovery hearing.

After about as much posturing and stalling as the plaintiff's lead attorney could come up with, the judge finally laid into him.

"You've wasted a good hour and a half of our time now. Do you have the document or not?"

I saw my client's victory all over his face.

"No, sir, we do not have that document at this time."

A whoosh of breath escaped me as I turned to Hamid. His face was covered in a giant smile, and he looked at me like I'd performed a miracle. Which, of course, I hadn't at all. Still, it was always nice winning for the client, and I leaned in to accept his outstretched hand for a shake.

It wasn't until exiting the courthouse in downtown San Jose that I turned on my phone and felt it practically vibrate out of my hand with messages.

My stomach dropped right away. That many messages could only mean some kind of bad news, and I was almost afraid to look at the screen.

There were twenty-two missed texts.

Dante: *Noah's hurt. On way to hospital.*

Dante: *Hit his head, I think. Hayworth called.*

Pete: *Call me when you get out of court.*

Jasmine: *Fuck, call me.*

My heart hammered in my chest as I raced to the parking deck to find my car. My eyes continued skittering over the pile of texts as fast as they could.

Hayworth: *I'm at the hospital with Noah and he's asking for you.*

Dante: *They're at St. Vincent's. Heading there now.*

Tilly: *Your boy being rushed to ER. Not sure if he's going to make it. Get your ass there now.*

I almost tripped over my feet. Fuck the text messages, my fingers fumbled to call Hayworth. He'd been the only one to say he was actually there with Noah so maybe he'd be most likely to know what was going on.

"Luke, thank god," he answered. "Everyone said to call you since you're like Noah's family... or something?"

"Tell me he's okay," I barked into the phone. Two women in suits jumped nearby, and I waved an apology their way before closing my eyes and taking a deep breath to steel myself. "Hayworth, is Noah okay?"

"I, ah... I don't know. I mean, I think so. I'm so sorry, Luke. He... wait, someone... hang on."

I wanted to reach through the phone and throttle the guy. Instead, I found my car and peeled out of the deck, heading back to the city as fast as I could.

"Luke, sweetie?" It was Rebecca Marian.

"Rebecca, please," I croaked. "Just tell me he's okay."

"Yes, he'll be okay. He has a concussion and some bad cuts on his face, but they said he should be just fine."

I felt the tears come then—tears of relief maybe, but they poured out of me, and I had to dash them away to keep my eyes on the road.

"He's been asking for you, Luke," she said quietly. "I think you should come straight here."

"I'm already on my way, but I'm coming from San Jose so it's going to take me at least an hour."

"That's fine dear. I'm here and so is everyone else. Don't rush and get yourself hurt too, alright?"

"I'll be careful," I lied. "Rebecca... tell him I'm coming okay? Make sure he knows I'll be there as soon as I can."

"I already told him that, honey."

It was the longest sixty-eight minutes of my life.

26

NOAH

I lost track of how many times I made a pathetic, passive-aggressive attempt to get the noisy fuckers out of my room, but there finally came a time when I just decided enough was enough.

Thankfully, someone had dimmed the light in my room so I could open my eyes fully. My head still screamed in pain though, so I spoke as firmly as I could without shouting.

"I need all of you to leave, please," I said.

The room fell silent. Had I been focused enough to be able to count, I was sure the number of Marians would have reached the double-digits.

All of those eyes stared back at me, and I sighed. "Look, I love you all. You've been amazing, and I couldn't ask for a better surrogate family. But you're a hot mess in large numbers. Surely, you know that. And, well, my head is fucking killing me. So here's what I need."

I swallowed and braced myself to say the words.

"I need Luke. That's it. Just Luke. And the rest of you need to hit the road."

There was shuffling behind the curtain in front of the door before it folded out of the way, revealing the one person I wanted. He was dressed in a gorgeous dark suit but the tie was askew and his hair was wild. His eyes were red rimmed and his face was pale, but he was still the most beautiful person in the room.

I exhaled and closed my eyes.

Finally.

His voice was strong and firm, taking charge despite the worry and exhaustion written on his face.

"You heard the man. Everyone out."

I smiled and let myself slip away again, knowing with Luke there to watch over me, it was okay to let go.

I DON'T KNOW how much later it was before I opened my eyes again. The pain in my head still made me wince, but I was able to open my eyes without wanting to vomit.

Luke's large hand engulfed mine on top of the blankets next to my hip, and his other arm was bent into a makeshift pillow beside it. His eyes were closed.

"Hey," I said softly, testing whether he was asleep.

His head popped up, and he stared at me for a second before his face softened. He squeezed my hand. "Hey, beautiful. How're you feeling?"

I felt my eyes fill at the question. "Bad," I admitted. "Really bad. It hurts."

He straightened up and reached his free hand out to gently wipe the tears away. "I'll ask the nurse for—"

"No," I said, clutching the hand I held so he couldn't take it away. "Stay. Please."

He shifted to find the electric keypad wrapped around part of the bed. "Ta-da," he said triumphantly, pushing the nurse's red call button. "Nobody's going anywhere. Just rest, baby. I'm right here."

I couldn't take my eyes off him.

"Thank you for coming," I said quietly.

His entire heart was visible in his eyes. "Of course I came, Noah. I will always come when you need me. Always."

I wanted to tell him that I loved him, that I always had, but I knew I wasn't strong enough to risk getting rejected again, especially feeling as poorly as I was. So I just smiled at him and tugged on his hand a little.

"Will you lie down with me?" I asked. "That chair looks awful."

"You sure you won't be too uncomfortable? It's a small bed, and I'm a big guy," he teased, his smile punctuated with a wink.

Instead of answering, I scooted over to make room. He'd already stripped off his jacket and tie, so he simply removed his shoes and socks and slid into bed, wrapping his arms around me and pulling me against his side.

He smelled so fucking good, like a man after a day's work mixed with the faint, fading scent of his familiar aftershave. I tucked my face into his neck and let the smell and the steady thrum of his heartbeat relax me back into sleep.

THEY LET me out of the hospital the following morning under the stipulation someone would keep their eye on me. Before I could open my mouth, Luke told them he'd be taking me home to his place and staying with me. When I complained to him, insisting he probably had work to do, he wouldn't brook any arguments.

"My big case finished yesterday and most people are already taking off for the holiday break anyway," he explained. "I was actually thinking I might pick up a small tree and decorate it while you sit your lazy ass on the sofa and watch."

"This close to Christmas? You can probably find a Charlie Brown tree on clearance at the tree lots," I teased. "Do you even have lights and decorations?"

I sat on the edge of the hospital bed while Luke helped me dress. He squatted down in front of me to place my feet into the legs of my jeans. It was impossible to ignore his warm hands on my skin and the look on his face as he looked up and caught my eye.

I gulped.

"My mom sent me a box of family decorations a while back. They're around the apartment somewhere," he continued, as if he didn't look like he was crouched down to give me head.

My heart raced so fast, I was glad I didn't have any monitors attached to me any longer.

"I can go stay at Dante's if it's easier—"

Luke stood up and leaned in until our noses were almost touching. "Noah Layton Campbell, shut the fuck up. You're coming home with me. We already discussed this. If I had it my way, you'd move back in with me anyway." He mumbled that last part while he turned around to find my shirt, but I heard it clear as day.

He still wore his suit pants and button-down shirt, only now they were a wrinkled mess. He'd put back on his shoes and socks and had the rest of his things folded neatly in the chair.

After I put on my shirt, he reached into the hospital bag for my coat and other belongings.

"Why is your jacket ripped?" he asked, looking at the frayed fabric where several down feathers poked out.

"Oh, Hayworth said one of the guys who knocked me over skated right over the top of me to keep from falling. Thank god I had my puffy coat on," I said, reaching for my socks.

Luke's face paled. "Are you fucking kidding me? Did they get the name of the guys who did this to you? Did Hayworth file a police report? Did—"

I reached out my hand to grab his wrist, wincing at the effect the quick movement had on my head. "Easy, tiger. It was kids being assholes. Not thugs intentionally assaulting me."

His jaw tightened. "You could sue them."

I almost laughed. "For what, their skateboards and vapes? They were kids, Luke."

He crouched back down to put my shoes on, grumbling the entire time about teenagers needing to be more considerate of the people around them. I almost pointed out that he sounded worse than Granny and Tilly, but I refrained.

Finally it was time to go. He straightened up and held out his hand to help me up.

"Let's go home. You'll be able to rest better there. This place is awful," he muttered.

While I agreed with him at the time, he turned out to be dead wrong.

The following days leading up to Christmas brought visits from almost all the Marians, including several of the men I'd been out on dates with. It was a dizzying parade of guests, and if I hadn't been busy trying to stay relaxed, I would have cackled at the annoyed look on Luke's face every time someone got too close to me or was overly affectionate.

Even Dante noticed it one day and leaned in to whisper in my ear. "Let's make it a game. Every time that vein pops out on his forehead, I'll steal you another cookie from the special stash Mom brought over."

"He's just annoyed people are in his space. I should move back to your place," I said, even though it was the last thing I wanted.

Dante smirked at me. "You're cute but mistaken. It's straight-up jealousy that other people are nurturing his man. The guy's in love with you. I'm surprised he's able to leave you long enough to go visit his family for Christmas. He flies out tomorrow, right? After we leave for Napa."

I nodded, glancing back over at where Luke stood hovering nearby. His eyes were locked on Hayworth and Jordan. The two men seemed to have met each other and struck up a conversation about cats. Luke looked like he wanted to kill one or both of them.

"It's not love, but clearly he's miffed. What's his problem?" I muttered. "It's obvious those two are into each other, not me."

"His problem was when Hayworth came right in with an armful of flowers and hugged you for an overly long time. And then Jordan asked Luke when you'd be back to work selling Love Junk. I thought Luke's teeth were going to break from all the jaw tightening that was going on," Dante said with a chuckle. "Watch this."

He scooted right up close to me on the sofa and pulled my legs into his lap, reaching out to begin massaging one of my feet. He raised his voice enough to be heard by my menacing roommate.

"God, Noah, you have nice feet. I mean, look at that. Masculine, strong, clean... I could rub these feet all day. They're cold though. Poor thing."

I noticed AJ's head turn from where he stood talking to Rebecca near the kitchen. His eyebrows furrowed until I caught his eye and winked. Then he smiled and shrugged before turning back to his future mother-in-law.

Luke, on the other hand...

Now that was a different story. His face went rigid and stormy right before he strode out of the room.

Dante laughed. "Got so mad, he ran away? That's no fun."

But no more than one minute later, he came storming back in and made a beeline toward me.

"Here, put these on," he snapped, thrusting a thick pair of wool socks at me.

Oh my fucking god, maybe Dante was right.

Maybe Luke Holland cared about me more than he wanted to admit.

27

LUKE

It seemed like every time I turned around, someone else was touching him. Sometimes they were innocent hugs, sometimes more. Some guy named Julio from the club came by to check on Noah and wound up trying to snuggle with him to watch a movie.

Knowing Noah, he'd agree to the snuggle just to keep Julio from feeling uncomfortable, but *I* didn't have the same reservations. Just as I was getting ready to plonk myself right down between them on the sofa like a jackass, I heard Noah speak up.

"No, thanks, Julio. I think I'd rather just rest if you don't mind. Rain check?"

I blinked at him. He'd been doing that more and more, surprising me with his newfound confidence to stand up for what he wanted instead of feeling like he had to please others. Yet he still managed to do it politely and with the Noah sweetness everyone loved so much.

"Sure, man, no problem. Another time." Julio grinned. He leaned over to peck Noah on the cheek.

"I'll walk you out," I said quickly.

I heard Dante laugh from somewhere near the kitchen and by the time I returned to Noah's side on the sofa, Dante had brought in a plate of Rebecca's cookies for him. The two of them chuckled softly.

"What?" I asked.

"Nothing," Dante said.

Noah's eyes were bright and mischievous. "You were jealous."

"Yeah? So?" I said.

Dante stared at me and slowly stood up. "I'm gonna head home," he said quietly. "I'll pick you up in the morning, Noah."

Noah and I gazed at each other across the sofa, hardly noticing Dante's departure. Once the door closed behind him, we were alone in the apartment.

"You're jealous?" he repeated. Only this time, it was a question, not a statement.

"Of course I'm jealous, Noah. I've been telling you for two weeks how much I want you."

His eyes went from teasing to sparking mad as he bolted to his feet. "Yeah? Well, fuck you, Luke. I've spent my entire fucking life wanting you, and when I finally thought I had a chance to do something about it, you bailed. Now that other men are paying attention to me, you finally want a piece of me too? Too bad. I don't need that half-assed bullshit. I deserve better and we both know it."

I stared dumbfounded at him.

"Wait, let me explain," I said. *Could there be a more pathetic line in the entire universe?*

He shot me an angry, exasperated look but waited for me to speak.

"I... I..." I took a breath to calm down. "Noah, please sit down for a minute and let me tell you something."

He sat back down but stayed on the edge of the seat as if ready to bolt at a moment's notice.

"When I went to university, I dated a man named Sid."

"I remember," he said. "Scott thought he was a jerk."

"That's because he slept around on me the entire time we dated," I explained. "And then I dated a guy named Andrew and he did the same. And then a man named Jon, and... you get the idea."

"What the hell? Are you trying to tell me you're attracted to assholes? Because that's not helping your case, to be honest," he said with his chin jutting out a bit.

"No. Every time in every one of those relationships I expected the guy to be monogamous, told them I wanted someone I could count on, someone who would be just for me. And do you know what they all said?"

He shook his head.

"That I only *thought* I wanted a commitment. They each told me in their own way that I didn't see them. That I treated them like just another side bit to my life. They claimed hockey was more important, or my classes, or law school, or my job. And the worst part about it? None of them seemed to mind. They were perfectly happy having me when I wanted and then having others when I was busy."

I rubbed my hands up and down my thighs. "So I began to think they were right. That I wasn't relationship material. One of the guys, Jon, actually said that most gay men just don't do committed love relationships like that. He was older than I was, so I thought he somehow knew more than I did. I was an idiot."

Noah nodded. "Yeah, you were."

"But it was easier, Noah. I have to admit that these past fifteen years of school and practicing law were so busy I didn't really have time for more than a quick fuck. And quite frankly, I didn't think I needed more." I took a breath. "Until you showed up and made me wonder if I had it all wrong."

"You did," he whispered. "Still do. Good night, Luke."

He got up and disappeared to his room, leaving me to stare after him with a heavy heart, wondering where I'd gone wrong and if it really was too late to convince him to give us another chance. I was leaving the following day to fly home to spend the holidays with my aunt and uncle, and he was going to be with the Marians in Napa.

28

NOAH

Christmas Eve at the vineyard with the Marians was the most fun I'd had in a long time. There was food and booze everywhere, and holiday music played from hidden speakers somewhere in the large vaulted lobby of the lodge.

The room was the family gathering place. There was an enormous stone fireplace lined with stockings and surrounded by several huge sofas and overstuffed chairs. The tree was lit up in all its glory, and the kids were busy poking curious fingers at the mountains of wrapped gifts under the tree.

I wasn't able to drink, but I still enjoyed watching everyone else get happily tipsy. Dinner had been an Italian feast, which they said was tradition since the expected American turkey dinner would be the following day on Christmas.

After gorging myself on lasagne and garlic bread, I offered to hold Blue's baby Mattie, otherwise known as the Terror. For some reason, she calmed whenever I held her, so I was pressed into Mattie duty quite often.

A ball of fresh mistletoe had been hung in the arch between the main lobby and the sunroom and various Marian couples kept "acci-

dentally" ending up there together and making out. I had to admit to
a little jealousy.

I still wondered if I'd done the right thing in expressing my anger
at Luke. I'd hated hearing about the assholes he'd dated, but c'mon.
Who could possibly think there was no such thing as a monogamous,
fulfilling relationship between two men? He was making excuses, and
I wasn't going to listen to it anymore. The truth was, he was terrified.
He finally had feelings for someone, real feelings, and he was
running scared.

And until he could admit that to himself, things between us were
doomed before they even started.

I looked up when I heard the front doors of the lobby open. Tilly
and her senator came in, flush-faced and laughing. Senator Cannon
held Tilly's arm in his as he led her to a seat near me and offered to
take her coat back to their room. I'd heard a rumor that he had Secret
Service protection, but I hadn't seen anyone since I'd been there. It
was hard to believe Tilly was dating the father of a sitting US
president.

My gaze wandered around the room and saw how many other
accomplished people there were. The Marians were a smart and
talented family. From Jude's music career to Jamie's animal research
to Dante's work with LGBT youth, they all seemed to have something
special to contribute to the world.

I'd enjoyed sitting next to Maverick and Beau at dinner. They
were very much in love and ended up telling me the story of their
second-chance romance.

Mav's eyes had lit up when he'd looked at his husband. "He was
the cutest fucking kid. All skinny legs and scabby knees."

Beau had let out a hearty laugh. "Shut up. You were cuter. That
dark hair was always overgrown and floppy. Plus, you knew the best
place to find crab in the creek."

"Still do," Mav had said, reaching over to pull Beau's chin in for a
kiss on the lips. Once they'd gotten their fill of each other, Mav
turned to me. "So, I heard you went out with my replacement at the
vet clinic, Jordan."

I laughed. "Yeah. He seemed a little more interested in my Love Junk than my personality, if you know what I mean."

Granny had piped up from her spot on the other side of Beau. "Can you blame them? That shit is premium. You brought my Lady-wax, right?"

I'd swallowed my sip of water, careful not to let it go down the wrong pipe. "Yes, ma'am. You left me three voicemails and sent two texts."

"Damned straight," she'd muttered. "Maverick here mentioned wanting to try out the Fornicator. You bring one of those?"

Maverick's eyes widened. "What the hell is a Fornicator, and why would I want one when I have one of my own?"

Beau had blushed to the tips of his ears. "Shut the hell up, Mav," he'd said under his breath. "Is it hot in here or is it just me?"

Mav's look had been feral. "It's for damned sure *you*. Smoking hot."

I hadn't been able to take any more of the lovey-dovey shit so I got up to clear my place and wander over to the bar area to pour myself a soda or something more than ice water. When we'd finally moved back to the lobby to lounge around the fire, I'd sat close enough to Simone and Joel Healy so I could eavesdrop on their whispered conversation.

Now there was a development none of us had seen coming.

Apparently, Simone and the bodyguard had barely spent a moment apart since our pizza date. After realizing how comfortable they were together already, I began teasing them.

"Simone, I don't know about here in the States, but in Canada, we don't steal people's dates right out from under them," I admonished.

Her face turned pink and she smirked. "Losers, weepers, Noah."

Joel looked at Simone like she was a magical unicorn until my words sank in. "Wait, what?"

I looked back and forth between them. Apparently, so did Teddy because he laughed his ass off and opened his big mouth.

"Simone was trying to set you up with Noah," he told Joel.

Joel turned to look at me in confusion. "What?" Then he looked at Simone. "What?"

"I told you that already," she insisted.

Joel looked surprised. "I thought that was a joke! You thought I was gay? For real?"

Simone tried to placate him through her laughter at the same time the entire clan was ribbing her for making such an obvious mistake.

"You told me he was gay," she cried to Derek and AJ.

Derek held up his hands. "No, sister. I said he liked cock. There's a difference."

Joel's laughter rang out in the open space. "Simone, honey, if you want to know whether I like cock or not, we can talk about it in private. Let's just say I'm glad the date ended up the way it was supposed to. No offense, Noah."

"None taken," I said with a grin. "I'm sure Simone's brothers take great pride in knowing her gaydar is on the fritz."

And they did. They totally did.

Tristan wandered over to check on his baby daughter who was dead asleep on my chest. "Time for bed, baby girl," he murmured. "It's Dad's turn with you tonight, sweetheart. I'm pretty sure you wore Papa out with all that screeching you did this afternoon."

Despite his words, he picked his daughter off my chest with the gentle hold of a man head over heels in love with his girl. By some kind of miracle, the crazy thing stayed asleep as he laid her against his shoulder and held her face into the crook of his neck.

"Thanks, Noah. Rest up. I have a feeling you're going to be on Mattie duty again tomorrow," he said with a wink before walking over to where Blue lifted Ella off Tilly's lap in a similar manner. The poor little girl had only just settled in when Tilly and Senator Cannon had returned from their walk.

Once the two of them exited the front doors with Tristan's hand on the small of Blue's back, Pete reminded his girls that Santa didn't come until all kids were safely tucked away in bed. Chloe and Hazel hugged everyone good night and made their way down the guest room hallway to the room they were happy to call their own. It made them feel like grown-ups when they were able to share a hotel room all by themselves. The fact that it connected via a door to Pete and Ginger's room was immaterial.

Once all of the kids were gone, Tilly's crew started a bridge game at the table off to the side of the Christmas tree. They convinced the senator to be the dummy even though from the sound of it, he'd had the winning bid. Typical.

I'd finally had the chance to meet Thad, whose laid-back personality was contagious. He proudly introduced me to his fiancée, Sarah, who it turned out was a doctor in the hospital where I was going to work.

After making my way over to where Sarah and Thad sat snuggled up together on a sofa, I asked Sarah to tell me about how she liked the ER in the hospital. But before she had a chance to answer, the doors to the lobby slammed open again, bringing the cool draft and making everyone jerk with the sudden noise.

The man silhouetted in the doorway looked like a psychopath. His eyes were wild, his hair was unkempt, and he wore a sweater that seemed to be covered in Santa gnomes.

"Luke?" I asked in surprise.

He strode across the expansive floor of the lobby until he caught sight of me. His arms waved about aimlessly at his sides like he was trying to come up with the words but couldn't.

Until he did.

"I love you, dammit," he cried. "I didn't think I could, but I do. I can't get you out of my fucking mind, and it's not even about me. It's about you. I want to make you happy, make sure you're not hurt, provide for you and... shit. I don't know. I just... I love you, okay? I want to be with you and I want you to be with me. You belong with me. We belong together. How many times do I have to say it to convince you I really mean it?"

The entire room fell silent and stared at the madman in front of me.

It felt like the entire thing was happening to someone else. My lips were numb, and I couldn't feel my feet.

"Um, once?" I said in a shaky voice. "Once is good."

He took the last few steps to reach me and engulfed me in his embrace, tightening his arms around me and shoving his face into my neck with a sob.

"I love you," he said. "I love you so much, Noah. Please say you'll give me another chance. I can't stand being without you."

My arms wrapped around him too, one hand going into the back of his dark hair to hold his head tight to me. I kissed his ear. "I love you too, Luke. So fucking much."

"OPAH! I win!" Ginger screamed, jumping up and down like there'd been a Powerball match.

"Goddammit," Pete muttered. "I'm never going to hear the end of this now."

Granny cursed and Tilly demanded a recount. Teddy called out something that sounded like, "Double or nothing on the wedding."

Money changed hands more times than I could count, and I didn't even care.

I had Luke Holland in my arms.

It was a Merry Christmas indeed.

TRYING to stay in the lobby with the Marians and be any kind of decent company for anyone was a lost cause. It didn't take long for Luke to mumble, "Fuck this," under his breath and grab my hand to lead me to my room.

Once we were behind closed doors, he turned and pushed me up against the door.

"You're mine, Noah," he said in a low voice.

I nodded.

"Say it."

"You're mine," I said obediently.

His face split into a beautiful grin. "That is also true."

I thought back to what I'd said and corrected my statement in a breathless whisper. "Yours. Always have been."

Luke's eyes darkened and he looked at me like I was filet mignon. I shuddered.

"I have a question though," I admitted as Luke's fingers busied themselves removing my clothes.

"Hmm." He was too busy gazing at my lips to pay much attention to what I was asking.

"Why Santa gnomes?"

He looked up at my eyes in a daze. "Huh? Because you like them."

"I do?"

"You have them on your underwear."

I thought about the pair of underwear he was referring to. "Oh." I laughed. "They were a dollar in the after-holiday sales last year. I got a bunch. My favorites are the—"

His mouth landed on mine, forcing the breath out of me, and all thoughts disappeared in a puff of smoke.

"I love you," he murmured, moving his mouth from my lips to my ear and down the column of my neck. "I love you, I love you, I love you."

My breathing was ragged and I wondered if my knees could continue to hold me up against that door. My cock was hard and weeping in my pants, and I silently begged Luke's fingers to work faster.

"Please," I moaned. "Please."

His lips lowered to latch onto one of my nipples and suck it into his mouth, causing me to hiss.

"I fucking love it when you beg," he said in a hoarse tone. "Drives me fucking crazy."

"Don't tease me, Luke. I want you so badly."

He straightened back up and cupped my face with his hands. "I know, baby. Tell me what you want. Anything, it's yours."

"I want you inside me, on top of me," I said, panting. "Looking at me. Kissing me. Touching me... *Jesus.*"

His face softened into a smile before he kissed me again, this time placing his hand gently on my throat again the way he knew drove me mad.

"Noah, just know that if you want to fuck me sometime, we can do that too. I want to make you feel good regardless of how we go about it, okay?"

His words were like adrenaline shots straight into my cock and I was dizzy with blood loss to the brain.

"Uh-huh," I managed.

"Is that 'uh-huh I'd like to do that now, Luke' or 'uh-huh another time, maybe'?" he asked with a grin.

"Second one," I breathed. "Please fuck me. Want to feel you inside me."

His strong fingers stroked along the cords of my throat in time to the throbbing in my dick. I finally began sinking toward the floor, held up only by his muscular thigh between mine and the hand on my throat.

"Take off the rest of your clothes and get on the bed, Noah."

I did as he said and lay on my back like a naked starfish. Luke took his time stripping, perusing my body with his eyes the entire time in an effort, no doubt, to drive me absolutely batshit crazy.

"Hurry the fuck up," I finally blurted. "You're teasing me again, dammit."

He tried to hide his smirk but failed. "I love teasing you, baby. You're so beautiful when you beg me. You like it too; I know you do. I can see it in your eyes and the way it makes you breathe heavier."

He was right. Of course he was right. I loved him taking charge in the bedroom, and I especially loved him teasing me. The anticipation and slow-foreplay session made it a thousand times better than a quick release.

I reached for my cock. If I was going to wait, I was going to enjoy it.

"Nuh-uh," he said, shaking his head. "Mine."

Two could play the teasing game. I clasped one hand around my opposite wrist and stretched them as far up toward the headboard as I could, bowing my body up from the bed in an exaggerated display.

Even though my eyes were closed, the sharp intake of Luke's breath was unmistakable.

My cock jumped, and he hissed again.

Gotcha, I thought.

"Naughty, naughty Noah," he murmured. I felt the bed dip and opened my eyes to see him propped above me. His face was flushed, and his lips were dark red from the kissing earlier.

"I love you," I said.

His entire face transformed beautifully.

"Thank you," he said. His hand skimmed my abdomen and upper thighs, coming back up by way of my balls and giving them a slight tug. I bent my knees and spread them farther apart. "That's it, Noah. Just like that. Open for me."

He moved down my body to take my cock into his mouth, and I cried out his name. From there it got a little hazy.

29

LUKE

Sucking Noah's cock and hearing my name pour from his lips was euphoric. After several bobs up and down, I moved off his dick to the hole below. I sucked and swirled until his fingers were tight in my hair and his words made no sense at all.

Finally I grabbed the condom and lube from my wallet and suited up before returning to my place between Noah's legs.

He was already half blissed out and panting where he lay on the bed.

Fucking gorgeous.

"You ready for me, baby?" I asked with a wink.

"*Mmpfh.*"

"Thought so," I said with a chuckle against his bent knee by my face. My lubed fingers danced along his prostate and cum dribbled from the tip of his cock. I could have done that all fucking night long. Played his body like a piano and found just the tune that drove him insane.

But when his begging turned to true whimpers, it was time.

"Please, Luke, please." His voice hardly even made a sound when he said it; he was so far gone.

I lined my cock up with his perfect tight hole and began to push.

Jesus fuck, he felt good.

"Luke, Luke," he panted. "Luke."

I leaned in and kissed him lightly on the mouth. "Here, baby."

"More," he breathed. "Want to feel you."

I slid gently in and out a few times until I sensed him relax further, and then I began to thrust for real.

"Ah, god!" he cried out, clutching my ass with his fingers. "Yes. God. *Fuck.*"

His body's tight clasp around my cock felt like heaven, and I had to grit my teeth to keep from coming right away.

"Mm, you feel so good," I groaned. "Noah, baby, shit. I can't... I can't..." I quickly grabbed his cock, stroking it firmly and twisting at the top the way he'd seemed to like when we'd had sex before. Apparently he liked it because his eyes rolled back in his head and his entire body arched up from the bed.

His release went fucking everywhere—on his chest, on my chin, on his shoulder. Finally, the last bit dribbled onto my hand and I brought it up to my mouth without thinking.

One taste of his salty fluid along with my dick in the vise of his orgasm made me go face-first into my own climax. It hit me out of the blue, and I could hardly catch my breath. My balls were tight and tingly, my cock was hard and jerking in his channel, and my voice cracked on his name.

Once it was over, I collapsed against his chest, heaving in breaths and shuddering from aftershocks.

Noah's fingers played in my hair while his heart thundered under my ear.

"I can't believe you came here for me," he said quietly.

I lifted my head to peer at him.

"You deserved better than my half-assed attempts," I admitted. "The truth is, I was terrified. What would have happened if we'd dated and it hadn't worked out? What if we got together and you figured out I wasn't the great guy you seem to think I am? I felt like the odds were stacked against us."

"It could still happen," he said with a teasing grin.

"No. I don't care. I'm not letting you go, no matter what," I promised him, kissing him under the chin. "I promise, Noah. No running. You're stuck with me now."

Noah grinned at me. "Okay, but get up. Unless you want me literally stuck to you."

We got up and took a quick shower together, rinsing off and enjoying the feel of each other's soapy hands on one another. When we finally slipped back into bed, Noah curled into my side like he was meant to be there.

And, of course, he was.

30

THE MARIANS - CHRISTMAS MORNING AT THE VINEYARD

"Aunt Tilly, goddammit. What the hell are these?" Griff glared at his great aunt from his spot on the floor next to a mound of crumpled up wrapping paper. He held up the bedsheets she'd given him.

"Weiner sheets," she explained in a bored tone. "Simone said the old wieners on your bed had shrunk. I asked her if she was sure she was referring to sheets, but she insisted she was." She shrugged.

Sam laughed at his husband. "She's not wrong, Foxy. Your wieners were looking awfully hang dog. Kinda rode hard and put away wet, you know?"

Griff turned to his traitor of a partner. "They were *your* goddamned sheets! I only inherited them by marriage. I never even liked them. And besides, these have dicks on them, not dachshunds."

Tilly flapped her hand. "Potatoes, po-tah-toes."

It was mid-morning on Christmas and most of the kids' presents had been unwrapped and strewn all over the damned place. The youngest of the babies had already been put down for morning naps and the older ones played with their haul in corners of the large space.

Simone was snuggled up against Joel's side, gazing lovingly at a tiny firearm he'd given her that morning. The handgun was dainty, if you could use such a word, and yet there was no one in that room who didn't keep one eye on her despite Joel having tried to reassure everyone he hadn't even brought bullets for it to the vineyard.

"I just think you should go put that thing in your room," Thad argued. "Bullets or not, you're going to hurt someone with it. And there are kids in here."

Sarah nodded in agreement from her spot next to him. As a surgeon in the city, she'd no doubt seen her fair share of bullets.

"Thad," Simone spat. "Go fuck yourself. You'd better be glad there are not bullets in it, or else you'd be the first I'd—"

Rebecca cut in. "Sweetheart, Thad's right. Maybe you want to put that where the kids can't get to it."

Simone's face returned to its softer state as she turned to kiss Joel before getting up to head to her room. "Okay, but isn't it sweet that he wants me to be able to defend myself?"

Jude let out a *pfft* sound. "Joel, you losing your touch? You once told me as long as I had Derek, I didn't need my own weapon."

Joel grinned and stretched his neck to make sure Simone was out of earshot. "It's an Airsoft gun. Only shoots plastic pellets. I just couldn't resist it when her eyes lit up at the outdoor store. She was so freaking cute about it, wanting me to teach her how to shoot."

Several of her brothers groaned, but Dante grinned wide.

"I totally get it. When AJ took me to the range and stood behind me to position my grip right, I learned what all the excitement was about. I'll take a shooting lesson from him any day of the week and twice on Sundays."

AJ barked out a laugh and pulled Dante's head close for a kiss to the nose. "Anytime, cutie pie. Anytime."

Joel looked back toward where Simone had disappeared. "Ah, maybe I should... ahhh, go check on her," he said before swiftly following her down the corridor to their room.

Granny muttered from her spot at the puzzle table. "He wants something stuck to his pants."

Sam got down on the floor and knee-walked to find a small gift under the tree for Griff. After finding a box about the size of a three-ring binder, he returned to the spot next to his husband on the couch.

"Open it, Griffin," he said softly. His eyes were worried and his brows furrowed.

"Sam?" Griff asked unsure. "You okay, sunshine?"

"Well, it's kind of a bittersweet thing," he began as Griff pulled off the paper and opened a box that was filled with paperwork. "I wanted to find your brother Ben for you for Christmas."

Griff's eyes snapped up in surprise, but Sam held out a hand. "Wait. Wait. I didn't find him exactly. I hired a private investigator and we got as close as the agency your parents used."

He didn't get anything more out for a few moments because Griff grabbed him and pulled him into a tight hug.

"I love you," Griff said into Sam's shirt. "God, I love you so much. Thank you for trying."

Sam sniffed and rubbed tears out of his eyes. "They said he can find you if he wants to— he's always been able to. And I made sure they had all of our current contact information. Hopefully one day..."

Griff ignored his own tears to thumb a few stray ones off Sam's cheeks. "It'll happen if it's meant to, baby. Thank you. In the meantime, we have Benji, yeah? We have our own family."

Sam's sister, Lacey, stood up from where she'd been helping Chloe and Hazel with a craft set. She hugged both Sam and Griff and told them how much she loved them.

Jamie elbowed Teddy and tilted his head toward a stack of gifts under the tree. "Do something. Cheer everyone up."

Teddy jumped up and presented everyone with the framed photo of Thomas and Rebecca he'd selected from the shots he took of them a few weeks before.

It didn't stem the tears.

Thomas was the one who cracked first. His fingers skimmed the glass of the frame. "She's so beautiful," he murmured before turning to Rebecca. "You really are. You're the most beautiful woman I've ever met."

Blue started sobbing, Tristan glared daggers at Teddy for upsetting his man, and Jamie began laughing at all of them.

All the while no one noticed Noah and Luke had been missing the entire time.

Because they had many, many things stuck to their pants.

EPILOGUE

NOAH - THE FOLLOWING SPRING

I wasn't even fully through my apartment door when the man attacked me. Suddenly, it felt like four pairs of hands were on me—grasping, clawing, roving, pawing.

He slammed me up against the door and wrenched my messenger bag off my shoulder before leaning in to take a bite out of my lips.

"Jesus fuck, what the hell's gotten into you?" I gasped through the nibbles to my lips.

"Want to fuck you right now, right here. Take you up against this door," he growled. My scrubs were already being shucked off and my clogs were kicked in opposite directions.

"Okay, I'm on board, shit," I gasped, letting it happen.

Luke's hands reached into my boxer briefs and grasped my cock, teasing it from the semi I'd sprouted at his first touch into the full-on monster cock it became once sexy times were imminent.

"Haven't seen you in weeks," he snarled before trailing his tongue up my neck and biting my earlobe.

"It's been two days," I corrected without thinking.

"Two days too long. Hate the night shifts when I have court in the morning. You need to quit. Or I do. One of us."

His mouth kept toying with my skin until I was sure my coworker Tabby was going to tease me so hard when she spotted my millionth hickey. But fuck if I cared.

I reached for his belt and realized he was only wearing underwear.

"What the hell? Where are your clothes?" I wondered.

"No clothes. Sex. All the sex."

He spun me around until my face was against the cold door and my palms were flat on the surface next to my face. I fucking loved it when Luke got like this.

"It's been so long since we've done it... what if... what if my hole's too tight?" I used my innocent voice—the one that sounded naive and blushing.

"Fuck," he muttered hoarsely from behind me. I had to bite down on my lip to keep from grinning from ear to ear.

"You won't hurt me, will you?"

"Jesus, fuck." More muttering.

"Maybe... can you, like, use your fingers first or something? Stretch me out a little?" I wiggled my ass back and forth as a familiar plastic bottle hit the floor and bounced across the room. It sounded empty. "Hey, wait. Is that our last bottle of Buttjuice?"

"No talking," he said roughly. I heard him pause for a moment. "But yeah, order more. That shit's perfect."

His fingers rubbed the stuff deliciously against my hole, sending zings of pleasure through to my balls until I was up on my tiptoes in anticipation. Thank god I didn't have to wait for a condom anymore. We'd ditched them officially back in February when I'd moved in and I didn't miss them one bit. We had lube stashed in places all over the condo and packets always in our wallets. If we wanted fucking, we got fucking.

"Please," I breathed against my will. I hadn't wanted to give him the begging this time. I was playing coy, not desperate. But we both knew the truth. I was desperate, and moreover, I begged for his cock every single time he lubed it up and pointed it at me.

His hands grabbed the globes of my ass and pulled them apart.

"So fucking hot. God, Noah."

I loved hearing him like that, guttural and turned on, breathless and bossy.

Once his cock entered me, I moaned against the door. "Yes. Fuck yes."

Luke's entire body pressed against mine, and his tongue came out to tease the shell of my ear as his thrusts pinned me to the door. His hips slammed against my ass with every thrust and my grunts became garbled.

"I love you so much, baby," he cooed into my ear. "Want to make you feel good."

I reached back with one hand and clasped the back of his head to hold him close.

"Love you too. Fuck, gonna make me come, Luke!"

It wasn't long before I painted the door as my orgasm slammed through me, sucking away my breath and sending surges of relaxed energy through all of my muscles. It seemed to go on forever, and I knew my own climax would pull Luke's out as well.

"Fuck, fuck," he stammered before arching his hips into me and thrusting into me as far as he could. I felt the warmth of his release as his cock jerked inside me, and when he pulled out, I felt dribbles begin to slide down my thighs.

Luke's forehead was tilted into my back between my shoulder blades. "If you could see how fucking hot that is. My spunk coming out of your body," he said in awe. "Christ, Noah."

I turned around and wrapped my arms around his neck, grinning at him like a fool.

Luke grinned back, rubbing his nose against mine before speaking. "Hi, honey, how was work?"

I thought about telling him about my crazy shift in the ER—the one where Dr. Ethan Rhodes had a mysterious patient who not only looked just like Griffin Marian, but also happened to have Griff's phone number in his pocket. Ethan had promised me he'd take care of it, but I couldn't help but want to reach out to Griff to let him know about the guy.

Ultimately, I decided it could wait until morning. The patient was in rough shape and clearly wasn't going anywhere. And meanwhile, I had a hot date with my boyfriend and Cary Grant.

"Tell you later. What's for dinner?"

Luke shot me an evil grin. "Spicy sausage. Sam gave me the recipe."

~

Want more stories set in the Marian world? Check out Made Marian Shorts *and* Made Marian Mixtape*!*

LETTER FROM LUCY

Dear Reader,

Thank you so much for reading *A Very Marian Christmas*, the seventh book in the Made Marian series! Don't miss the accompanying short story collections, *Made Marian Shorts*, which features four tales of beloved side characters finding their very own HEA. And *Made Marian Mixtape*, which features some of Aunt Tilly's backstory as well as Ammon's romance novella. Ammon was the young man AJ saved and delivered to Dante.

If you haven't already, please check out my Forever Wilde series, beginning with *Facing West*. It's set in the same world as the Made Marian series and begins with the story of Griffin Marian's best friend, Nico.

Be sure to follow me on your favorite retail site to be notified of new releases, and look for me on Facebook for sneak peeks of upcoming stories.

Please take a moment to write a review of *A Very Marian Christmas*. Reviews can make all the difference in helping a book show up in searches.

Feel free to sign up for my newsletter, stop by www.LucyLennox.com or visit me on social media to stay in touch.

To see fun inspiration photos for all of my novels, visit my Pinterest boards.

Finally, all Lucy Lennox titles are available on audio within a month of release and are narrated by the fabulous Michael Pauley.

Happy reading!

Lucy

ABOUT LUCY LENNOX

Lucy Lennox is the creator of the bestselling Made Marian series, the Forever Wilde series, and co-creator of the Twist of Fate Series with Sloane Kennedy and the After Oscar series with Molly Maddox. Born and raised in the southeast, she is finally putting good use to that English Lit degree.

Lucy enjoys naps, pizza, and procrastinating. She is married to someone who is better at math than romance but who makes her laugh every single day and is the best dancer in the history of ever.

She stays up way too late each night reading M/M romance because that stuff is impossible to put down.

For more information and to stay updated about future releases, please sign up for Lucy's author newsletter on her website.

Connect with Lucy on social media:
www.LucyLennox.com
Lucy@LucyLennox.com

WANT MORE?

Join Lucy's Lair
Get Lucy's New Release Alerts
Like Lucy on Facebook
Follow Lucy on BookBub
Follow Lucy on Amazon
Follow Lucy on Instagram
Follow Lucy on Pinterest

Other books by Lucy:
Made Marian Series
Forever Wilde Series
Aster Valley Series
Virgin Flyer
Say You'll Be Nine
Hostile Takeover
Twist of Fate Series with Sloane Kennedy
After Oscar Series with Molly Maddox
Licking Thicket Series with May Archer
Licking Thicket: Horn of Glory series with May Archer
Honeybridge series with May Archer

Visit Lucy's website at www.LucyLennox.com for a comprehensive list of titles, audio samples, freebies, suggested reading order, and more!